THE DEATH OF JOSÉ

A WESTERN FRONTIER STORY

EVERETT RIGGS

RUBY VALLEY PRESS

*To my wife and son, the Gonzalez family, and
Roberto and Margaret.*

FOREWORD

This is a work of fiction. Although I depict actual events and real people in the book, the reader should take nothing written as historical fact. Any actions or dialogue are purely the creation of the Author, and any resemblance of said actions or dialogue to actual events is coincidental. This book is more than a simple recitation of history.

That being said, there was a real man, José Pizanthia, who died a horrific death at the hands of vigilantes in Bannack, Idaho Territory (now Montana) on January 11th, 1864. His death followed on the heels of the hanging of Sheriff Henry Plummer and his deputies the previous day. We know little about the real José. I learned about his death as a young man, and I have always wanted to give him a story. I invite the reader to study this period of Montana history, as it is fascinating, and there are many lessons to be learned. Draw your own conclusions regarding the actions of the vigilantes.

If you, the reader, ever travel to Bannack, climb up the hill to the old graveyard. If you listen carefully, you might hear the old ghosts whisper, "There are many kinds here. Many kinds."

1

ARRIVAL

The land does not forget the deeds committed upon it, and neither rain nor time can wash away blood and death. On quiet days, the wind will whisper these deeds into your ear if you listen.

JOSÉ STOPPED his horse and looked down into the valley at the mining camp of Bannack.

The wind was in his face, blowing away the smell of dirt, horse, and leather. Taking in a deep breath, José looked at the view before him. Mountains and sky, burnt grass, sagebrush. A green strip along the creek below.

It was early August 1863, and José clutched the reins in one hand, his other resting on his Colt Navy. Removing his hand from the revolver, José leaned forward to pet his horse on the neck; it had been a loyal companion all along the trail, and José held a genuine fondness for the animal despite not giving it a name. It was a big, muscled bay with good breeding, a horse that worked hard and did not easily spook.

The beast had a sullen attitude, however, as though it was not entirely happy with its lot in life. The steed never failed to make its views known, but despite that, its perpetual bad mood never adversely affected its steadiness. In any case, José did not mind the horse's constant moaning; in fact, the animal's attitude amused him, often making him laugh as he rode.

The horse even seemed to begrudge carrying its master, though young José—only in his mid-thirties, and thin and wiry—barely could have registered as a weight upon its strong broad back.

Anyway, José could hardly take issue

with the horse's relentless huffing about its burdensome problems since he also wore a scowl on his face most of the time, although it was fair to say this was not his true nature; it was a mere mask, the same mask that most wore when they had spent much time in wild and rough places.

But he was not without humor and was known to be kind to those in need.

José had grown up in the borderlands of Texas and Mexico, near El Paso del Norte, enjoying an upbringing of relative comfort for the area, and he had rarely known true poverty. He had obtained an education and was fluent in the gringo language, as people called it in his home village. The desire for adventure and wandering had led him to the mining camps, and the trail from Salt Lake City to Bannack was what had then brought him all the way to his current spot.

He had not been alone on the journey; a group of freight wagons was alongside, providing safety and companionship when traveling through wild country. Bandits and Indians were the dangers foremost in travelers' minds on the trails, so at each stop for the night, the wagons would form up into a corral, ensuring all stock and people were on the inside of it.

The corral formed a good defense against any danger posed by man or beast; because of this, most people would try to get a sleeping spot underneath the wagons. If it rained or snowed, and if luck came their way, that person might even find a place under the canvas on the tops of the wagons. There was no respite for anyone from the guard shifts throughout the nights, each traveler having to take their turn on watch duties.

Disease, however, was the one trail danger against which the corral could not offer protection, bringing a far more signifi-cant and real danger than men or animals could pose.

On this trip up the trail, José had already seen a young man die from fever, taking the whole of three tormented days for the man to die in a fit of delirium. Much of that time, he had spent alone in a cramped spot in the back of a wagon. There had been no time to pause, no time to stop to wait for the sick man to recover or die. They could not do a thing for him, could they? So, what would have been the point in holding up progress for everyone else?

After all, there were no doctors in the traveling caravan, and the available medicine had most likely come their way via a traveling salesman, so perhaps it was not all that reliable. Living or dying on a journey of this sort was a roll of the dice, and only the Creator knew the outcome.

When the man died, José helped dig the grave.

They dug it deep enough to keep the animals away, but no deeper than that since it was an effort and hot work.

The men heaved the body into it, having first wrapped it in a dirty piece of canvas. They filled the grave with dirt, stacking large rocks on top, then fashioning a simple wood grave marker out of a loose board in one of the wagons. José, being one of the few literate people among the group, roughly carved into it an epitaph about the man despite the fact they knew so little. It was better to write something than to leave him only with a name.

Then, they anchored the marker into the grave, one man said a prayer, and without further ado, they doffed their hats and moved on up the trail.

In that forlorn spot, the young man would lie until time and weather erased the words on the board. In time, the board too would rot away, only the earth knowing of his existence.

The trail was not all fear and tragedy. Each day brought some new sight, and the nights were often clear and full of stars. José would sleep out in the open in the middle of the corral, gazing up at the night sky to bring him comfort and sleep. One night, he saw a star shoot across the sky, making him think of his mother. A shooting star was a soul being carried to heaven, she had said, and it was true; there had also been such a star on the night José's beloved father had died.

The freighters were rough men but excellent and friendly trail companions. The skill of the bullwhackers impressed José as they coaxed and directed the teams of oxen pulling the wagons. Their big whips snapped in the air, and the oxen begrudgingly obeyed, even though they were in no better a mood than the ill-tempered horse.

Around the campfire, there was always a

song or a story as they passed around a bottle of whiskey to the thirsty—or to those who just liked a hard drop of liquor to round off an even harder day. Indeed, the days passed quickly on this trip, and the whiskey had played its part.

José tapped the big bay with his feet and slowly began to work his way down the hill into Bannack, where there was movement and activity in the town. He had always liked the bustle and air of expectancy that hung over a mining camp. There was gold to be found and fortunes to be snatched from the earth. People scurried here and there, worrying they might miss something if they stood still too long. Drinking and merriment were always present, but also sorrow and despair. There was grinding, hard toil which they set against rest and companionship which they found in the saloons or the company of a woman if someone struck lucky.

It was always different and always the same. José would move on before the lethargy of ordinary life or the inevitable decline of the diggings brought the party to an end. But on this day, there was only newness and the excitement of things to come.

José rode onto the dusty main street, passing rough buildings made of logs; some had facades, while others were just long rectangular log cabins built in a rush to separate the miners from their treasures. A few canvas tents stood here and there among the buildings. The inhabitants of the camp immediately noticed all newcomers, and José felt many eyes on him as he moved up the street, feeling the stares of a group of women standing outside one of the rough log cabins.

As he neared the group of women, a tall, lean blonde-haired woman in a once fancy but now old and shabby dress stepped forward. She called out, "Hello, José!" She waved to him, then added, "I haven't seen you in a while. Actually, I was quite worried about you. You're arriving a bit late to the diggings, don't you think?"

José rode up to her and stopped, tipping his hat in an exaggerated way, with a grin.

"Hello, Sally. You look as lovely as ever. To tell the truth, I've been slightly late my whole life. But I always seem to find a little dust wherever I go. I even find a nugget every now and then."

Sally put her hands on her hips. With a

smirk, she said, "Get down off that horse and visit us for a spell. The girls and I are lonely. You look like you could use a stiff drink and some companionship."

"I would like to, Sally, but I'm a little short on dust at the moment. I haven't laid eyes on any actual money in some time."

"Well, José, if we're talking about an honest man like yourself, I might be willing to give you some credit."

"No. No. I plan on visiting you quite a bit after I get established. Credit has never been a good thing for me. I don't want to get myself into that mess."

"Then you had better get to work, hadn't you?" She laughed and then became serious. "You're always welcome to stop in for a drink and a visit. You know that. I never did thank you for getting me that doctor back in Colorado when I had the fever and was in a bad way. You left before I could so much as thank you."

"It was nothing, Sally. I was just helping a fellow traveler in this world. It was my pleasure. Have you seen Wichita Dan or heard of him being in these parts?"

"Wichita certainly is here. We see him

quite often when he has dust to spend. His claim's up the creek a bit. Just follow the main street out of town and follow the trail along the creek." She pointed the way. "Ask around, and someone will show you where he's working."

"Thank you. I'll do that. See you and the girls soon."

"We'll be waiting for you."

José nodded to Sally, waved goodbye to her and the girls, and started his horse up the street.

He'd only gone a few feet when he noticed a young woman standing between Sally's building and the next. The woman was wearing a plain cotton dress with a brightly colored shawl wrapped around her shoulders and couldn't have appeared any less like Sally and the girls if she'd tried. José was confused by her presence so close to Sally's establishment. What would such a woman be doing here? It wasn't usual.

He stopped his horse and stared at her.

She looked directly at him, and he noticed her bright, shining eyes. She had long, soft black hair hanging down past her shoulders and she wore it unbraided, gently swaying in the wind. Her face was beautiful and angular, with exotic high cheekbones.

The woman's demeanor was neither inviting nor alluring, but it was also not cold or standoffish. She looked familiar to him, but he could not place how he knew her or where they might have met before. Still, José was sure that he did know her.

His unease was obvious, and this seemed to amuse the woman. She smiled at him, a look of warmth and familiarity, one that certainly confirmed that she knew him. She suddenly said, "Hello, José."

"Hello." Now, he didn't know what to do or say. "I...I'm sorry, but I don't remember your name." What he really wanted to say was that he had barely any recollection of her; it wasn't only her name he had forgotten with the passing years.

"My name is Marina."

"Oh! I have a sister with that name. I love that name. I last saw her when she was just a little girl, many years ago."

"Really?" Her eyes widened in mock surprise. "That isn't a good thing. Why has it been so long since you've seen her?"

"I honestly don't know why it's been so

long, but you're right. It isn't good. But about you and me... When did we first meet? You look so familiar to me. We know one another, don't we?"

The smile left her face and she stared at José intently, a look of sadness coming over her while she remained silent. Several seconds passed, the two of them looking at each other while neither spoke. José decided that he needed to go, needed to get away from this strange young woman, the one he thought he did not know and yet somehow recognized.

He quickly said to her, "Have a good day, Marina. I have to go now. Maybe I'll see you again sometime."

"Maybe you will, José." Her face remained expressionless. "Maybe soon."

José put his head down and urged his horse forward, careful not to look at Marina again. He did not know that she was no longer there.

2

CAMPFIRE

José followed the trail out of Bannack and up the creek, his thoughts turning to finding a claim and a way to survive. He took in the activity along the creek, mounds beginning to form on both banks of the stream. The miners were moving large amounts of dirt and gravel, searching for the precious yellow metal. José began to worry about finding a claim.

He was late to Bannack as it was, and there didn't appear to be much available. Certainly, other miners had already taken the best spots. He put the negative thoughts aside, having always found something that paid in every camp he'd inhabited. Just the same way, something would turn up in Bannack.

José asked several people along the creek if they had heard of Wichita Dan and his whereabouts. Eventually, a miner directed him to Wichita's claim, and as he rode up, he could see the bent-over figure of Wichita working in the creek. Wichita wholly absorbed himself in his work and clearly didn't notice José riding up to him on the horse.

José called to him, "Hey, Wichita? What are you looking for? Finding anything interesting?"

Wichita stood up quickly and turned to face José with a look of surprise. He was a medium-sized man, fit and muscular. Wichita always wore clothing that one would expect to see on a businessman in town, except it was dirty and worn from hard work. He was clean-shaven and wore a short-brimmed hat. Only his boots fit in with his chosen profession.

He shook his head and said, "I'll be damned. José. It is good to see you. Your horse looks a little tired. Did you wear him out rushing to Bannack?"

"This is a good horse. It never gets tired. You know I am always well mounted. Maybe when there is not much money or gold, the horses aren't too good. I have been known to walk."

"A Mexican walking in this country... better be fast."

José laughed. "That might be true. I am not fast on foot, but I am stealthy. That might be more important."

"Being stealthy is worth something. Anyway, the day is late. Do you have anywhere to bed down for the night?"

"No. I just arrived in the area."

"You are welcome to stay here. I have a little dried meat to put in the beans tonight and a bottle of whiskey. I also have another surprise for this momentous occasion. I've done pretty well here so far."

José nodded in approval. "Since you offer such a feast, I must accept. Thank you, my friend."

Wichita pointed to a small tree near José. "You can get your saddle and gear off that horse and tie the horse there. I will get to work on the meal."

José took the tack off the horse and took

the animal down to the creek to water it. He then took the horse to the tree and tied it with a long rope so that the horse could graze. He took his saddle and propped it up against a log close to the fire. José sat down and watched in silence while Wichita prepared the meal. Wichita quickly cooked the food, and soon both men were heartily eating. The hot meal provided great comfort. José finished eating and said,

"Damn, Wichita. That was delicious. You must have learned something about cooking since the last time I saw you. Thank you."

"You are welcome. Now take a tug on this bottle."

Wichita tossed José a bottle of whiskey. José pulled the cork, took a swig, and handed the bottle back to Wichita. They carried on like that, just passing the bottle back and forth between them, each man taking a couple of drinks, then handing the bottle back.

Then Wichita said, "Now, for the surprise." He reached into a sack and pulled out a tin can, handing it over to José. Well, that was something new!

José looked at the can, his eyes widening.

"Oh. Canned peaches. What a treat! You certainly must have been doing well. But I don't know if I deserve something this valuable."

"Seeing a good friend is always a reason to share something precious. Come on, let's eat them."

José handed the can back to Wichita, and he opened it. They both took turns savoring the sweet juice in the can, sticking their fingers inside, bringing out the juicy chunks and savoring them one by one. When they finished eating, they both sat in silence, reveling in the pleasure of their treat. The day was quickly fading into dark, and Wichita threw some more wood on the fire while both men stared at the dancing flames, watching them flicker into the shapes of monsters, beasts, and men.

José flicked a small stick into the fire and said, "Wichita, what do you think my prospects are around here? Are there any decent claims left?"

"I think I can put you onto something. Things are still burning pretty hot in this camp. Are you willing to work for wages?"

"Yeah. That's no problem. I need a little

start to get going. I want to be hunkered down and comfortable when winter arrives."

"I'll ask around and see what I can turn up. Hey...I don't think I ever asked you this, but how did you become a prospector in the first place, José?"

"I don't really consider myself one. I think of myself as an adventurer who prospects to find more adventure. But I left home shortly after my father died, just after I turned nineteen. My mother took up with another man, and I couldn't stand him, so I left. I had a sister, Marina, who was almost ten at the time. That's what I remember the most, that it was sad to leave Marina there. But what could I do? I could hardly drag my sister along, could I?"

"Do you ever write to them or see them?"

"No. I haven't seen either my sister or mother since I left. Seems so long now. But I still think about them a lot, especially in these lonely places."

"Lonely! What? You feel *lonely?*" Wichita pushed his hat back on his head. "José, there are people all around us in these camps."

"Yes. There are many people, but it still feels lonely. To me it does, anyway."

"Sounds like you may be suffering from melancholy. A doctor might have something to fix that up. You should go see one. No point in suffering through this life feeling glum, is there?"

"Maybe, but I stay away from doctors as much as I can... Anyway, like I said, I think about Marina the most. When I last saw her, she was just a little girl. We were close, even though our ages weren't. She was a beautiful girl. When she was happy, her eyes would twinkle, and she'd have a big smile that would always bring you joy. How could you not smile?"

"She had big dimples in both cheeks and freckles to go with them. It's a rare thing to see a smile on such a pretty face." He was wistful now, tears pricking at his eyes. There was only one thing he could do. "Pass me that bottle, please."

Wichita handed José the bottle, and he took a long drink, the whiskey beginning to take effect on him. He held the bottle up to the light, looking at it with something akin to adoration.

"Looks like we're going to run dry soon," he proclaimed, looking as if even that thought had set off his melancholy. "That's one experience I don't want to re-live. Unfortunately, I ran out of whiskey a while back on the trail. Anyway, I don't mean to drink up all your stash."

Wichita waved his hand in the air. "Don't worry about it. I have another... There's always another bottle where that one came from. How did your father die? Was it violently?"

José shook his head.

"No. He died of sickness. Terrible, it was, at least at first. It took him a day to die after he went to his bed. I sat with him a lot during that time and would hold his hand to give him comfort. He would drift in and out, his eyes would glaze over, and his breathing turned ragged.

"I thought it was the end several times, but he'd always come back, you know? You couldn't keep my father down even in his final days. His mind would clear, and his breathing would become steady. Sometimes, he'd stare off in the distance and talk to people I couldn't even see. But like I say, his mind was clear, so he really believed he was seeing them!

"Other times, he'd ask me if I could hear people singing. I couldn't hear them. He had one foot in this world and one foot in the next. Then, he just stopped breathing, and that was that. I honestly think he saw something he liked better in the other world, and he decided that was the place to be. So, off he went."

José emptied the bottle. Wichita retrieved another bottle of whiskey, pulled the cork, and took a long drink. José got up and threw a piece of wood on the fire.

"What about you, Wichita? Do you have any family out there in the world? It's strange that we've never talked about these things before, isn't it?"

Wichita never answered that, already thinking of his reply to the first question.

"I had a wife and son, but they met a bad end." Wichita looked off in the distance. "A wagon accident. The horse went wild and turned the wagon right over, toppled it. I was at the reins. I tried to stop the horse, but I couldn't stop it before things went bad. I was hurt in the accident, but they were hurt too badly to live. Even the horse had to be shot since it was also hurt bad."

"I am sorry, my friend."

"Yeah. They didn't die right away either. The boy went first. His mother knew it, and it made her suffer even more. Finally, she passed away. I have never been able to get over them lying there, so still. I wanted to shake them and make them wake back up. But, of course, they never did."

"I understand the stillness. I saw this with my father. When death first comes, for a while, you can still feel warmth in the body. Once the eyes close, they almost look like they're sleeping, don't they? You keep thinking it's not real and soon, everything will be the same as it was before.

"But, you know, deep down, that isn't true because the skin starts to become splotchy and lose its color. More time passes, and they lose more color. The jaw grows ever wider, and they look unreal. Like a shell, and you realize that the person you once knew has really left you forever. And yes, the terrible stillness. It presses on you like a weight."

Both men sat there, each in their thoughts, partially in shadow and partially in light, the crackling of the fire and the hum of the night creatures setting off against their silence. José snapped a twig in his hand in two.

"Wichita, what do you think happens when we die?"

Wichita rubbed his chin and thought for a moment. "I guess...I believe what the Bible says. We either go to heaven or hell. I don't know if I will see my son or wife in heaven one day. I may not make it in, but I sure know they are there. That thought makes me happy. What about you?"

"I didn't use to believe in anything, Wichita. I thought everything just went black, and that was the end of things. But I've thought more and more about my father's death as the years have passed and what he experienced before he died. Now, I believe there is something more after we die. Someday, I will get to see it."

"You will... That's a guarantee. We all will see it."

José had paused. "As I've been traveling these wild places, I've seen our Creator's work. On a clear night when the stars are bright in the sky, and in the cool shade by a stream, watching the water bubble and wander over the rocks. When the sun first brings the morning light over the mountains. Have you ever found anyone since, Wichita? You know, since your wife and son passed on? Someone that you loved?"

Wichita looked up and thought for a moment. "No...Not really. I'm not sure I can feel that way again. I've been out on the trail and in these camps too long. There was only one woman for me, and the Creator decided to take her away, so what can I do except work till the day He joins us back together? Anyway, that's enough about me. How about yourself?"

"Oh, I've known many fine women in my day," said José. "I just thought of a famous Mexican bandit that I once knew when I was a teenager as well. I even had a couple of drinks with her. She was a tall, pretty woman. Very elegant and intelligent. The people called her The Desert Flower. Do you want to hear her story?"

"Sure, why the hell not? I'm always inclined to hear one of your stories."

José began, "She told me that a relative left her money in a bank in Zacatecas, but the bank refused to give it to her due to some legal issue or other. She viewed this as a grave injustice and decided that the best way to make things right was to go and *rob* the bank!

"She dressed up in the shawl of an old woman and hobbled into the bank, managing to draw no attention at all until she was right there, at the counter. She then pulled out the pistols hidden beneath the shawl and robbed it. Can you imagine, an old lady packing pistols like that, in the bank? But yes, that's what she did! Then she fled out into the desert on a horse and hid out.

"The robbery went so well that she decided to make it her profession. And so it went on. Eventually, she moved up into the borderlands, where she was safe. She stayed in a small village close to where I lived and always helped the people. In return, they protected her from the authorities. That is where I met her. I was very enamored with her, in fact, and even felt I might be in love. One day, I heard that a robbery did not go so well for her, and that had me worried.

"There was a shootout, and she fled into

the desert and was not seen again. There was a rumor that she made it across the border and lived among the Texans. I don't know. I do like to think that she is still alive and out there somewhere. I remember her real name was Yvonne."

Wichita looked at José with a smirk. "That sounds like it might be a bit of a tall tale to me."

"No, Wichita. I can assure you that it is true as best I can tell it."

"Okay, but I asked you if you'd ever really known love."

José took off his hat and ran his hand through his hair. "I've been very fond of some women. I wouldn't call it love, but I did care about them a great deal while I was with them. But there was always somewhere else to go and something else to see."

He stopped and thought. "Before I left home, I knew an auburn-haired girl from across the river. Sometimes, I still think about her. I would sneak across the river to see her quite often, and we used to ride out into the desert and talk. We would take some food with us and stay out until the late afternoon. Do you know how the colors of nature get deeper and richer just before the sun goes down?"

"Yes. That is true." Wichita nodded in agreement. "I have always liked that."

"Well, when the time came just before the sunset, the last rays of the sun would make her auburn hair almost glow. I would look at her, and she would look away shyly and smile. And the colors of the desert would become magical. The world seemed to fall away, and there was just us. I cared about her a great deal at that moment."

"I know what you are talking about, José."

"What will become of us, Wichita?"

José's quick change of subject threw Wichita off and he didn't understand what his friend meant. He quickly said, "What do you mean, José?"

"We can't do this forever. Someday, we will be too old or injure ourselves. What do old men do in these kinds of places when they are alone?"

"Plenty. You see them around here every day, and they seem to do all right. Plus, a person could always move to an established town. You don't have to stay in any place you don't feel is right. Look around you; do you see any chains, keeping you here?"

"I suppose, but we aren't fit for town living. We like to wander too much. Someday, the wandering will have to end, one way or the other. Then what? What do you do when the things that sustained you are no longer there? I fear growing old and living in despair almost more than anything."

"I don't know what to say, José, other than it seems pointless to be worrying all the time. I don't think about it much. I think we stay at the table and play the cards we are dealt until the money runs out. Then we are in the hands of God. Don't you think, my friend?

"I like to think I will hit it big someday and have a nice house in a big town. Maybe have some servants. For now, I think we both need some sleep. But really José, try not to worry all the time about things that are outside of your control."

"You are right. To hell with it. Let's get some sleep."

Wichita went to the creek, got some water, and poured it on the fire. José untied a blanket that he had on the back of his saddle and settled in beneath it.

Wichita crawled into his bedroll, and both men were soon asleep. The night settled in around them. Both were dreaming of things from the past and things to come.

3

FALL

Pick and shovel. Grab the rocker box. Throw some dirt on the screen. You need a little water. Fill up the tin can ladle and pour it on the dirt. Get it good and wet. You need more water. Keep pouring it on the soil. Grab the handle on the rocker box. Rock it. Keep rocking and keep the water coming. Check the apron and riffles down below. They hold the gold. See any color? Yep. Then collect the gold and put it in the pouch. Get to work setting up the sluice box. Work. Work. The dirt is rich. You need to get that gold. It is life here.

José could not find a decent claim, but he

did find employment working for a crusty old character known as Old Man Dunphy on a claim up the creek from Bannack, near Dogtown. Dunphy was a forty-niner who started prospecting in the California gold fields at the very beginning of the rush. He was getting long in the tooth, and the hard toil over the years was beginning to show, so it was getting harder and harder for him to do the work.

Dunphy had been lucky to stake a good claim in the Bannack area and had lately taken to hiring men to help him work it. José happened to come along at the right time, and Dunphy knew Wichita and trusted his judgment, so he hired José straight away.

Dunphy had a long, white beard and hair, and always wore a wide-brimmed hat turned up on one side, and his clothes were worn and filthy. But his language, at times, was even dirtier than his clothes. Dunphy smelled terrible, and José was confident that he never bathed more than once a year. He took drinking and gold seriously, in equal measure, and anything else had to take the last spot on his list of things to do.

However, he was an honest man who paid well and always on time. José was grateful to have work and didn't mind Dunphy's rough ways because of that. Dunphy knew miners in the area and was an excellent source of information about anything related to prospecting or potentially available claims.

On a fine, sunny day in early September, José was busy working the sluice box when Dunphy announced, "José, I'm going to take a trip soon."

It seemed to be out of the ordinary for him to approach and just come out with something, so José stopped working, wiped the sweat off his brow, and looked over at him. Dunphy was sitting on the creek bank and had just pulled out a bottle for his first drink of the morning. José said to him, "Where are you going?"

"I am going down to Salt Lake City to make a deposit in one of the banks. I don't trust anybody around here, other than Christman over at the store, to hold my gold."

"That could be dangerous. I hope you're

not planning to go by yourself. Do you want me to go with you?"

"Oh, hell no, I'm not going alone. There are bastards around here that would like a crack at my gold. I heard some freighters were heading back to Salt Lake City in a couple of days, so I'll head out with them. I figured out how to sew most of the dust into the lining of an old jacket. I also have a secret spot to stash some on my horse, and besides that, I always keep a little in a pouch to hand over to bandits. It throws them off from searching for more. You stay here and work the claim. Take out your wages and put the rest in the safe at Christman's store."

"Okay, Dunphy. When will you be back?"

"I plan to be back in a little over a month. It's going to be a couple of weeks down and a couple of weeks back. I don't plan to linger in Salt Lake. I never really cared for the place, but the point is, I know my earnings will be safe there. I will join up with the first bunch heading back this way. I think you can handle things all right while I am gone."

"Sure. No problem. I'll do as you say. I hope the journey is safe and goes well for you."

"I don't have anything to worry about." Dunphy took a drink from the bottle. "I've been doing this a long time. They haven't got me yet, and I don't plan to let them. Hopefully, I'll fall over dead in a creek somewhere one of these days. That will be as good a way to go as any."

"Dunphy, as crusty as you are, you might live forever."

Dunphy let out a big laugh. José smiled and then went back to work.

Dunphy left as planned, and José settled into the routine of working the claim alone. He missed the company of Dunphy as the banter with the old man was always a source of amusement in an otherwise constant stream of hard toil. José did as Dunphy instructed him to, removing his wages in dust and taking Dunphy's share down to Christman's store to be put in the safe.

Many miners used Christman's store to safeguard gold before moving it to a more secure location. The miners believed the store to be as safe as a bank for two reasons. One, the owner, was universally well-liked and trusted by the community. Any attempt to rob the store or the safe would bring down the entire wrath of the community upon the perpetrators. Second, Sheriff Plummer maintained an office, in the form of a desk, in one corner of it.

The town had offered to build a small log cabin to house the Sheriff's office, but Plummer had refused. He maintained that his desk in the store corner worked well and saved the community money. Besides, he argued, the store was a community focal point, allowing him to interact more easily with everyone. José did not keep his savings at Christman's, nor did he tell anyone of his hiding spot, not even Wichita. He didn't trust anyone when it came to gold or money, and he always wanted quick access to it. Some would have thought José paranoid, but he viewed himself more as prudent. You never could be too careful in the camps.

The first part of October came and went without the return of Dunphy. Then mid-October passed, and still, Dunphy did not appear. José began to be concerned about the old man, but he was aware the trip to Salt Lake City was difficult, so any number of things could cause a delay. He put his concerns away and went about his business.

José had just purchased a small cabin from a miner who left for Alder Gulch. It was located on a hillside above Bannack, sitting in a natural flat spot. The place was one room, with a small chimney built into the middle of a wall. It was constructed of rough-hewn logs, notched on the ends, and stacked up to a height that was enough for a tall man to stand up inside, while the roof slanted from front to back to shed the inevitable snow. It had one small window with a pane of rolled glass. A sturdy door frame and door completed the structure.

Inside, José had removed the built-in bunk and made it into a movable bed. Supplies and personal items were either stacked along a wall or placed on the one shelf in the building, and two chairs and a small, old table furnished the interior. José was proud of it, and it was a nice cabin for a miner in Bannack.

He liked to sit in a chair outside the place and watch the sunset over the town when he had the chance.

When November arrived without the appearance of Dunphy, José immediately went to Sheriff Plummer, reported him missing, and asked for some assistance.

The Sheriff promised José that he would look into the matter. But it was a cool morning when the answer to the disappearance of Dunphy arrived in the form of Wichita Dan. Wichita arrived on horseback at the claim and whistled loudly. José stood up quickly, and when he saw who it was, he called out, "Hey, Wichita. Good to see you. What brings you here this morning? Shouldn't you be working?"

"I'm afraid I bear bad news." Wichita dismounted from his horse and started walking toward José. "They found Dunphy's body out on the trail just a few miles out of town."

"What? Who found him? He was supposed to be traveling with freighters. How could this happen?"

"It was freighters who found him. One of them saw some grouse fly into a patch of trees. He went after them in hopes of getting a tasty addition to the evening meal, but when he entered the patch, he noticed a pile of brush. On closer examination, that's when he saw a boot sticking out.

"So, he moved the brush and that was it; he'd found the body. The man called the other freighters over, and one of them who knew Dunphy identified the body by the clothing and some personal items. There was nothing of value on the corpse. But remember that old Sioux medicine bag he used to wear around his neck? That was on him."

"I do remember the bag. The damn fool must have taken off without joining up with the freighters." José was visibly upset. "Told me he wouldn't leave without them. He wouldn't go anywhere, so he said, not without the freighters. Now, look what's happened. I even offered to go along with him, and he refused."

"They dug a grave for him and buried him close to where they found him."

"At least he got buried. And after learning what you've just told me, I'm packing it in for the day." José shook his head, looking off into the distance "Let's go to Durant's Saloon and have a couple of drinks."

"That sounds good. Let's go sink a few for the old man."

José packed up his work implements, and the two men set off for the saloon.

November passed by quickly. José did not let the matter of Dunphy's death rest. He asked around town seeking information, and would stop in at Christman's to see if the Sheriff had learned anything. José continued working Dunphy's claim just as he'd promised, taking out his share for wages, and keeping Dunphy's for deposit. He began to entertain thoughts about taking over the claim, but he also wanted to make sure he did it legally so that no one could jump it.

It was a lot more likely that someone would jump the claim since everyone now knew that Dunphy was gone. He didn't know what to do, but he didn't think the other miners would go along with someone just jumping Dunphy's claim, so he also figured he would have assistance if that happened. In any event, José intended to fight for the claim, legally or otherwise.

In addition, José wasn't sure what would become of Dunphy's share of the gold now that he was dead. Dunphy had never spoken about any family that he might have, and in fact, he had never talked about any personal matters at all. Still, it seemed best to keep depositing Dunphy's share until things could be sorted out. He didn't want anybody pointing fingers in his direction regarding Dunphy's death.

In the last week of November, José approached Christman's store with gold that he wished to deposit. The cold was starting to set in, and he knew winter was close now.

Winter usually meant more time in the saloons and less time working, so José figured he had enough dust to get through the harsh wintertime. As José neared the store, there appeared to be a small man leaning up against the building. He walked up to the individual. Then he was surprised; it was not a man at all but a large boy wearing a bowler hat, and clothes too big for him. The boy also had a belt and holster appearing to contain a Walker Colt.

José looked the boy over from head to toe and said, "Good day, son." The boy stood up straight and puffed out his chest.

Then, he placed one hand on the revolver. José smiled slightly at this display and said to the boy in a kind voice, "How are old are you, son? Aren't you a little young to be sporting that pistol? You need to be careful around here. Some men don't have much sense of humor. It could be dangerous when they see you with that."

"I'm plenty old enough for this pistol, mister. I just turned twelve."

"Where is your father? Is he working a claim?"

"Nope." The boy relaxed a little and lowered his head. "He ran off with one of those fancy ladies. He left me and Ma in the lurch. I have to take care of things now."

"And your mother? Where is she right now? By the way, what is your name? Mine is José."

"My mother is in the store." The boy pointed to the store entrance. "My name is Kaleb. Christman put me in charge of guarding outside here, and the Sheriff also made me a deputy and said that I could wear my pistol as long as he was in the store at his office. When I'm not guarding stuff or being a deputy, I have to do other chores."

"I see. I haven't seen you here before. You must have just started."

"Yep. We just got started. Both Ma and me."

José looked at the store entrance and then back at the boy. "It looks like you're doing a good job in your guard and deputy work. May I go into the store?"

"Sure, mister." The boy waved his hand at the store entrance. "Go on in."

José touched a finger to the brim of his hat, nodded, walked to the door, and entered the store.

Once inside, José removed his hat and looked around, seeing a woman placing items on a shelf. She turned, looked at José, and smiled. He returned the smile. "I assume you must be the mother of the young deputy outside?" he asked.

"Oh, Lord." The woman shook her head in exasperation and spoke quickly, in a staccato manner. "Kaleb didn't cause you any trouble, did he? He can be a handful at times, but he doesn't mean to be trouble, but I know that he has been wearing some of his father's clothes and his pistol."

She looked anxious, barely pausing for a breath, then she set off again.

"His father ran off with one of the

sporting women around here. I heard they went to Nevada. It's been hard on him, you know, so Christman and the Sheriff indulge him a little bit. We are just grateful for the work. You know how hard it is."

"No. Don't worry. The boy was no trouble at all."

"Thank goodness. So, is there any way that I can help you?"

"There is, as it happens. I need to speak with Christman about some business. Could you get him for me?"

"Sure. He's in the back room. I'll get him right away." She hurried off to retrieve Christman before José could respond.

José heard the creak of a chair and looked in the direction of the sound. Sitting in a chair by the stove looking at him was Sheriff Plummer. José walked over and said, "Hello, Sheriff. Do you mind if we talk a little when I finish conducting my business with Christman?"

The Sheriff replied, "Sure. We can talk. Conduct your business and then come and warm yourself by the stove."

Christman and the woman returned from the back of the store. The woman returned to work, and Christman walked over to José. "José," he began. "I suspect you have a deposit you wish to make into the safe. Is that why you've come?"

"Yes, if you don't mind. How has your day been going?"

"As good as can be expected. Busy. You might have to make a trip to Salt Lake soon."

Sheriff Plummer perked up at the mention of a possible trip, and he looked over at the two men. His look was intense and serious, though neither José nor Christman noticed it. The Sheriff remained silent, listening closely.

José thought for a moment and said, "Yeah. I suppose I might have to take a trip there pretty soon, though I keep putting it off. I can't say as I'm looking forward to it after what happened to Dunphy."

"Truly, a shame." Christman grimaced as he thought about it. "I don't know what things are coming to these days. Well, shall we go to the safe?"

José and Christman went into the back room and returned a couple of minutes later. Christman went behind the counter, and José walked over to the stove. He stood close to it, rubbing his hands together, taking in the stove's glow and warmth.

"José, grab yourself a chair and sit down." Sheriff Plummer gestured to a seat. "Then, we can talk."

José grabbed the chair and placed it over by the stove. He looked across at Plummer with a grin and said, "Sheriff, it looks like you might be a little short on labor around here. I met your new deputy out in front of the store. They're getting younger and younger. But he seems confident enough."

Sheriff Plummer threw his head back in laughter. "Hell, José, things are tough around these parts. I need all the help I can get. Now, how can I help you?"

"I don't want to keep bothering you, Sheriff, but have you heard anything new about Dunphy?"

"No. I'm sorry, but I haven't turned up anything at all; the clues are thin on the ground. I do have my deputies making inquiries of course, but we haven't made any progress. You know how things are in the camps. People don't talk unless you force them to. But you can be sure we'll keep working on it. I understand you are still working Dunphy's claim?"

"Yeah. I've been working the claim. Staying busy."

"How are things going? Finding any color? You might want to take the claim over now."

"It's panning out nicely, you could say. Well, more or less. And yes, I *am* looking into taking over the claim. I don't know much about the legal part of doing it, and I want to do it right."

"Don't get too bogged down in the legalities, José. You might find yourself out in the cold. If you wait too long, somebody is likely to move in on you. I will help you in any way I can. You know where to find me."

"Thanks, Sheriff. I know how things are in the camps for a person like myself. Do you mind if I ask you a personal question?"

The Sheriff leaned back in his chair. "No. Not at all. Shoot away."

"How did you come to be a lawman in these parts? Did you always do this kind of work?"

"Ah, it's a simple story. I chase the gold just like everyone else around here. When I was in California, I started doing a little law work to supplement my earnings when the prospecting slowed. I found I had a knack for the job, so kept doing it whenever I needed the money. It was the same thing here. I arrived as a prospector and became a sheriff. Why, are you looking to become a lawman yourself?"

"No. No. I was just curious. I suppose I'd better get going. I need to get back to work. Have a good day, Sheriff."

"You too. If you ever see me in Durant's, feel free to buy me a drink."

José chuckled and replied, "I will do that."

José left the store, making sure to tip his hat to the boy standing guard outside.

José did buy Sheriff Plummer and his deputies a drink from time to time during the next month. They would sit in Durant's Saloon and swap stories about their adventures in different mining camps throughout the West. José enjoyed their conversations and the reminiscing. It was Sheriff Plummer who interceded on behalf of José one night when alcohol and poor judgment led to him breaking out some panes in one of the windows in Durant's. José ended up paying for the damage, and all seemed forgiven. But people hardly ever forget anything in the camps. Eyes are always watching and judging, calculating. Some of those eyes were watching José.

4

CHRISTMAS

I t was early morning on Christmas day. José dressed, grabbed a cotton bag filled with goods, and headed into Bannack. His destination today was Sally's cabin, and he had a spring in his step, in anticipation of the day ahead. Very few people were moving about, and José enjoyed the stillness. The sun had not yet risen sufficiently to clear the winter's morning haze.

José arrived at Sally's and banged loudly on the door. He heard movement inside the cabin, and then Sally called out, "Just a minute. Hold on. I'm coming." He waited patiently at the door, a little bit nervous but also excited. The door soon opened, and

Sally stood in the doorway with a sleepy look. She was still in her nightclothes, and her hair was unkempt.

She said to José, "Good grief, it's José. What brings you here so early? None of us were even awake yet. You know we don't normally conduct business at this hour."

José grinned. "That's because I'm not here on business. No work today, Sally. It's Christmas, and I mean to celebrate it with you and the girls."

Sally's face brightened. "That's right. It *is* Christmas. Come on inside. I'll get the stove going and warm this place up. I'll make some coffee too; I've just roasted some beans and ground them up."

"I also have some surprises, Sally."

"Really? What are they, José? I see you have a bag with you there. What's in it?"

"I'll show you when we get inside and the girls are out of bed and dressed."

Sally and José went inside the cabin. It was big for Bannack but drafty and not well maintained. In the front part of the place was a sitting area containing a threadbare red velvet couch that had long since seen better days. There were several wood chairs and a table too.

Wood planks, fashioned into shelves, were located close to the stove and contained bottles of alcohol and other household goods. A wood stove completed the front. The women resided in and entertained customers in the back part of the structure in tiny, cramped partitioned areas. The back area also contained an old bathtub. Privacy was, for all practical purposes, non-existent. Sally and three other young women were the primary residents.

José walked over to the table and placed his bag on it. He pulled a chair up to the stove and watched as Sally lit it. Before long, warmth began to seep into the room and spread throughout the cabin. Sally prepared the coffee pot, and soon it was boiling. José enjoyed the aroma of the brewing coffee and was eager to have a cup.

Next, Sally grabbed cups from one of the shelves, poured José and herself coffee, and handed him his cup. She pulled up a chair next to him. José let the cup warm his hands and then sipped the strong, dark brew. He leaned back in his chair and said, "Ah, that tastes good on a winter morning. Especially a Christmas morning. You make good coffee, Sally. I've never been able to get roasting the beans quite right. You just seem to have the knack."

Sally smiled. "Kind of you to say so, and I'm happy you like it. The key to roasting is to get the skillet at the right temperature. You don't want to burn the beans, so you need to put a drop of water in the skillet, and if it sizzles right off, you know you are at the right temperature."

"Then you stir the beans until you hear them crack. It's a smoky affair, so it's best you do it outside. But you know that. It sure is nice to have a genuine guest at Christmas. But I must say, I'm surprised you didn't receive an invitation to a proper house for Christmas festivities."

"This is a proper house for me, Sally. People like me don't get invited to Christmas dinner by the upstanding citizens. It's always been this way in the camps. Sometimes, a group of us miners would get together and have a meal or a celebration. But I have never received an invitation to a family's home for Christmas. It's okay though. Besides, I would much rather be here with you and the girls. Where else would I want to be?"

"That is sweet. If it makes you feel better, the upstanding citizens don't invite the girls or me to their houses either. I guess we're both in the right place."

They both laughed and then sat in comfortable silence, enjoying the coffee and the warmth. José took a drink of coffee, hesitated, and then said,

"Sally? Do you mind if I ask you something personal? Don't feel like you have to answer. Okay?"

"Sure. Ask away."

"How did you arrive in the brothels? I mean no disrespect. I've been wondering and was too afraid to ask you before."

"What gives you the courage now?"

"I don't know. I care about you and want to know your story. I can't say why, for sure. Now seems like the right time, and it's important to me to know more about you."

"I care about you too. It's okay. I'll tell you, but I might need to fortify this coffee."

She went over to one of the shelves and grabbed a bottle of whiskey. Sally poured a healthy glug into her cup and offered the bottle to José. He took it and did the same. She returned to her chair, took a long drink from her cup, and began her story,

"I was raised on a farm in Iowa over by the Big Sioux River. It wasn't much of a farm, and we barely fed ourselves. Mama was a hard worker, and Daddy was too at times. But he liked to drink and gamble, and eventually, he wanted to do it more than anything else. He said he was going to town on a Saturday, and he never came back. It was that simple."

"Did you ever find out what happened to him?"

"Nope, we never did. We tried to keep the farm going, but couldn't make a go of it. Mama decided she needed to stay home with the rest of the children, and so she made inquiries to find me a job in the nearby town. I was able to secure employment with a wealthy family doing domestic work. I was fifteen at the time. Would you please hand me that bottle, José?"

José handed her the bottle, and she poured more whiskey into her cup.

"The lady of the house was a mean one,"

she carried on. "Some silverware came up missing not long after I started working there. I was the newest domestic worker in the place, so suspicion fell in my direction. No one would take responsibility, which enraged the lady. The head domestic worker said I must have done it since I was new, and no silverware had been stolen before. She fired me and threw me out into the street. I was too embarrassed to go home, so I lived out in the street and did what I could to feed myself."

José patted Sally on the back, and she smiled at him. The story was not over yet.

"One day, a well-dressed lady saw me and asked me if I needed work. I said I did, and she took me to a house filled with other fancy ladies. Men would come and go at all hours. I started out doing domestic work there, and then she eventually coaxed me into the business side of things.

"She knew how to make it sound attractive, saying there was more money, less hours to work, and the clients were mostly easy pickings. I don't mean that as it sounds but more that they liked the girls and paid generously, especially after a good day.

"After a few years, I struck out on my own and ended up in the camps for the same reason we're all here, and you know what that is. Easy money. I saved some of it and have put together a group of girls who work for me. As you well know, we travel around following the gold. We don't stick to one place. I consider myself a businesswoman first and foremost."

José leaned over and kissed Sally on the cheek. "Merry Christmas, Sally. And yes, a businesswoman you are."

"Merry Christmas to you too and thank you." Sally paused. "José?"

"Yes."

"Do you think anyone could love me?"

"*I* love you, Sally."

"I know you do in your own way. But, I mean, could someone love me differently? Like, marry me and take me to a nice house?"

"Is that what you want?"

"I don't know. Maybe I don't know what I want. Sometimes, all I can see is blackness in this life, José, and I'm afraid it will swallow me up. I visit the celestials and smoke their pipe when I feel really sad about it all. It helps some, but there are still nights when I wake and can't get off to sleep again, worrying about ending up old and lonely."

Lonely. There was that same word José had used. Life *was* lonely at times; that was true. It was sad to think of poor Sally that way, and José reached out a hand to her and gently placed it on her arm. "You won't end up old and lonely," he reassured her.

"And as for smoking the pipe, believe me, Sally. I've done that myself. I think there are candles of light in all the darkness, and we have to keep traveling from candle to candle. Just keep going. I don't know, but I know I'm here with you today at Christmas, and that is a candle."

"It sure is, José. Now let's get those sleepy girls up and have a celebration. Is Wichita coming over?"

"No. Wichita got invited to a family's home for Christmas dinner. However, I'm sure he sends his regards."

Sally laughed. "I bet he does."

Sally got up from her chair and poured herself another cup of coffee, added a little whiskey again, and then in a loud voice called to the back of the cabin, "Girls! Get out of bed! It's Christmas, and we have a visitor. Put on your best clothes and come to the front. We're going to have a party."

Slowly, one by one, three young women appeared at the front area, dressed poorly but provocatively, their blossoming youth overcoming any deficits in their clothing. The first to appear, Alice, was tall and brown-haired, and looked as if she had just left the farm and had arrived at the cabin by accident. She was rail thin, and Sally constantly told her to eat more and gain more weight.

She usually was shy and didn't talk much, but alcohol dramatically overcame her shyness.

Next to appear was Beth, robust and curvy, beautiful and talkative. Her body was proportioned in a way that made her very alluring, and that, combined with her personality, made her popular among the band of girls as well as the men.

The last to arrive in the front area was a Shoshone woman, and everyone called her Sue. She had been the bride of a local miner who'd died in a drunken knife fight over a claim. Unable to support herself or return to her people, she had gradually found her way to Sally. Sue's personality was often outwardly flat and unemotional, but she was not unfriendly, and was pleasant to be around once she felt comfortable. The miners often sought her out.

Soon, everyone was clutching a whiskey, either in coffee or not, depending on their preference. The group became festive as the alcohol took effect, and attention soon turned to the bag on the table. Sally pointed to it and said, "Okay, José. It's time to show us what is in the bag."

José moved to the table and grabbed the bag. "Give me a moment, and I will show you. Patience, ladies. Patience. Everything good comes to she who waits."

He began removing items from the bag and placing them on the table slowly, one at a time to build up the suspense. Tins of meat and fruit were first, followed by eggs and a loaf of bread. Last out of the bag was—of course—a bottle of whiskey.

The women squealed with delight and clapped their hands, and Sally exclaimed, "Goodness! This must have cost you a fortune. Your prospecting must be going very well. But you must hold onto it, José; it's too much for the likes of us. Don't waste your earnings on a bunch of—"

"Nonsense. It's Christmas, and I've been able to squirrel away a little extra dust since I've been here. What good is all the work if you can't enjoy its fruits? And I promise you, there's no one I'd sooner share it with than all my friends here."

"We are surely thankful for this generosity, José."

José grinned. "Oh, and there's one more surprise."

José reached into the very bottom of the bag and pulled out four pairs of knitted mittens and four knitted scarves. The eyes of the women grew wide as they saw the gifts.

"I hope you like them, ladies. I had them knitted just for you."

José passed the mittens and scarves out to the women, and as he did, each one gave him a big hug and kiss. Sally had tears in her eyes, and she raised her cup to José, as did the others. Sally said to the group, "What a wonderful Christmas. I am so happy to spend it with all of you."

They spent the rest of the day drinking

and eating the food brought by José. That day, there was no work, just merriment and respite from an often harsh and unforgiving existence. Anyone who stopped by joined the party, and the day passed quickly, not a single visitor showing any disrespect to the women. The atmosphere was convivial, and the company animated and lively.

But even on this day of happiness, dark clouds were starting to gather around Bannack. José did not see them. No one did until the storm was upon them. By then, it was too late.

5

THE LIST

In the new year, 1864, two days had passed when James Williams and a posse of six men rode up to the main house at Rattlesnake Ranch. The men dismounted from their horses and took up positions on both sides of the door to the sprawling property.

Williams went directly up to the door and knocked hard on it. Three men readied their revolvers, and the other three messenger guns, shortened shotguns used on stagecoaches and wagons for protection. Williams carried only a pistol, and he now placed it tight against his chest, on the side, just out of sight of whoever came to the door.

He wanted to be ready but not cause undue alarm to whoever might appear.

There was no answer to the first knock, so he rapped against the door again, a longer knock this time. The door slowly opened, and Ned Ray appeared in the doorway. Ray had a pistol at his side, its barrel slightly raised but not in a way that suggested he intended to use it quickly. Williams backed up a couple of steps, and the other men moved into Ray's line of sight.

Once Ray realized the nature of the situation, he dropped the barrel on his pistol straight down and said, "What is your business here?"

Williams responded, "We are looking for Red Yaeger. We want to question him about the killing of Thiebalt by Ives. We think others might have been involved, and Yaeger might know something. We also believe he might know something about other criminal activities occurring in the area."

Ray sneered. "By what authority? I am a deputy around here, and if anyone questions Yaeger, I will be the one doing it. Did you clear this with Sheriff Plummer?"

"Sorry, Ray. A vigilance committee has

been formed over in Alder Gulch to look into this matter and other criminal activities going on in the area. I have been sent over here by the Committee to fetch Yaeger for questioning. I intend to carry out my orders, one way or the other."

Ray was silent, nervously glancing around at the assembled men. He then said, "Look, men. I'm not going to stop you because Yaeger isn't worth the trouble to me, though I don't approve of what you are doing. But you'll find him in a tent up the gully out back." Ray pointed, squinting. "Is there anything else you need? I will be telling Sheriff Plummer about your actions."

Williams gave Ray a stern look. "No. That will do for now. You have a good day, Ray."

Williams then turned to the men. "Mount up, gentlemen. We'll be on our way."

Ray closed the door quickly. Williams waited until the door closed and then walked over to his horse and mounted it. The posse followed suit, and they all rode their horses slowly around to the back of the ranch house and started up the gully.

The gully was an old, washed-out creek bed running moderately uphill. There were well-worn game trails on either side, so traveling upwards was not difficult for the horses. The lower part was mainly open with very few trees, bearing crusted, wind-blown snow on the ground, making travel very noisy. The open country and the crusted snow ensured that whoever was above them would know of their approach. They moved forward with great caution.

The men could see a stand of trees at the top of the gully in what appeared to be a small flat area. A thin tendril of smoke drifted lazily above the treetops, giving away the location of Yaeger's tent. The men were anxious as they moved closer and closer to the area.

They had reason to fully expect trouble from Yaeger.

Soon enough, the dirty canvas of Yaeger's tent began to come into view, and Williams halted the party. He put a finger to his lips to signal for silence and then gestured to the men to dismount. He got down off his horse and gathered the men around him.

Williams whispered to the group, "Three of us are going in on foot from here. The rest stay here and hold the horses. Be ready to get up to the tent quickly if there's trouble."

Williams pointed out the two men he wanted to take with him, armed with shotguns, and they continued up the trail.

Williams and the men slowed as they approached the tent. They stealthily inched forward until they were within shooting distance, only a few feet from the tent entrance. Williams could hear activity coming from within the shelter, and then it stopped. The entrance to the tent was simply a flap of material, and it was partially open. Williams gathered the men around him with a gesture of his hand. He whispered in one man's ear, "I will enter the tent first. Be ready to aid me." He then moved over to the next man, whispering the same instructions.

Williams rushed through the tent entrance, pistol held at eye level, cocked and ready to shoot. Yaeger sat on a wood stump in the tent with his back to the flap. He immediately turned to face Williams, who leveled his pistol directly at Yaeger's chest and said, "The game is up, Yaeger. Surrender. Don't make it harder on yourself."

Yaeger raised his hands. "Why are you here? Who are you?"

Williams kept his pistol leveled at Yaeger and called the men outside the tent to enter. The men quickly went in and covered him with their shotguns. Williams holstered his revolver and said, "Yaeger, I have come here on the orders of the Vigilance Committee formed in Alder Gulch. My name is James Williams. I am taking you back to the Gulch so that the Committee can question you about the death of the Thiebalt boy. We think there were others involved and that you might have useful information. We also believe all the killings and robberies in the area might involve an organized group and that you might know something."

Yaeger asked, "Can I put my hands down? I am unarmed at the moment."

"Sure. Go ahead."

Yaeger put his hands down and said, "I don't know a damn thing about any of those things. You can take my word for it."

"We will let the Committee decide whether or not you know anything. You are coming with us, Red. You can do it peacefully, or we can make things hard on you."

"I will come along peacefully. You won't have any trouble."

"Good. I am glad to hear it." Williams looked at the men. "Let's get him down to the others. Then, we'll head back to the ranch house for the night. We'll leave early in the morning and try to make it to Dempsey's."

In due course, they marched Yaeger down to the other men and the horses, forcing him to walk to the ranch house while the others rode. When the group arrived at the house, they discovered that Ned Ray had already left, and the place was standing empty. The men settled in for the night, Williams setting up a guard rotation for the prisoner so that Red would be under a watchful eye throughout the hours of darkness.

Early the following day, in the frost and haze of the morning light, they saddled the horses, and the group prepared to leave. They took a mangy thin-looking horse from the ranch corral and provided the bony steed to Yaeger, allowing him to ride without restraints, believing the horse was too weak to outrun the rest. Williams only hoped the horse would hold up enough for the group to make good time to Dempsey's, where they could obtain fresh mounts.

In January, the winter weather could be dangerous, and it was necessary to spend as little time on the trail as possible. A sudden snowstorm or a night exposed to severe cold could be disastrous. Freezing to death and frostbite were ever-present hazards along the way. The group traveled with speed until they reached the main route between Bannack and Alder Gulch. Then, they turned toward the Gulch and made it to Dempsey's without incident.

Dempsey's Ranch was a way station for travelers going to or from Alder Gulch. As such, it provided all the basic staples of travel, these being a place to lie down, warmth in the cold, and something to eat. The place did not emphasize comfort and variety, although alcohol was available to overcome these deficits. Upon seeing Williams' group enter the rough structure serving as the station, the bartender, a man named Robert Brown, looked up from his work. Brown was surprised to see Red Yaeger come through the door and said to him, "Hey, Red. What brings you this way on such a cold day? I will get a bottle out for you, and I have some boiled beef too. Perhaps you sensed it was in the pot."

Before Yaeger could say anything, Williams immediately responded to Brown, "How do you know Yaeger?"

Brown went quiet and looked around at the men in confusion.

Williams shouted out, "Get the drop on him."

They drew their guns and pointed them at Brown, who weakly put his hands in the air. Williams moved over to him and checked him for a weapon. Then he took a knife off Brown's person and removed a shotgun from behind the makeshift bar. Williams was now satisfied that Brown was not a threat. He gave his next command.

"You men move Brown and Yaeger over to a corner and stand guard with the shot-guns. Pay close attention. I know everyone is cold and tired, but we can't be lazy now. We have another man in custody. Who knows what else this day may bring?"

The men helped themselves to the boiled beef and some stale bread. They were all provided with whiskey and a turn warming themselves at the stove; Williams sat in a chair by its side too, deep in thought. He suddenly stood up and said, "Damn this thing. We need to question Yaeger a little bit. Bring him outside the building so I can talk to him. Make sure to tie his hands tight behind his back. Here's some rope. I don't want Red to think he can make a run for it. And more to the point, I don't want to hear that any of you let him do just that. D'you hear me?"

They nodded solemnly.

The men completed the task of restraining Yaeger, and the small group moved outside. Here, Williams began to question Yaeger relentlessly about people he knew and what they might know about the killing of Thiebalt. At first, Yaeger gave no helpful information, but as Williams became more insistent and threatening, Yaeger started to crack.

A man named Alec Carter and others had assisted Ives in the killing and attempted disposal of Thiebalt's body, he admitted. Thiebalt had a fair amount of gold dust on his person and had been openly bragging about it, making a vile habit of boasting in front of men who had barely anything. They had killed him to steal his gold. Well, what else did he expect for all his shows of ego?

Yaeger informed Williams that after Ives had been hung for the killing, he and Brown had been enlisted to warn the others involved to leave the area.

Williams was confused. "What are you saying, Red? Are you telling me that you are part of a group killing and robbing folks around here?"

Yaeger looked scared. "I'm not saying I am part of anything. I'm just telling you that Brown and I were enlisted to warn people. We didn't have anything to do with that killing."

"I don't know if I believe you, Red. You have to be part of a group or at least be in league with it for anyone to enlist you to do anything, wouldn't you agree? Tell me what you know. You must be part of something bigger. We think road agents are working in this area. We can't have that kind of thing happening. So, are they going to bushwhack us on the way to Alder Gulch or what's their plan?"

"I don't have anything more to say, Williams."

"Your choice, Red. But I will tell you, I'm starting to think I might have to hang you and Brown right here."

"I think you intend to hang me no matter what. Your mind is already made up. So, I don't have anything to say. I can't see how this is going to end well for me, no matter what I say to you."

"All right. We'll take you back inside. It's getting damn cold out here."

The group moved back inside, and Williams announced to the others, "Yaeger's confessed. He's also implicated Brown."

A man shouted out, "If he confessed, we need to string them both up right now. We don't need to wait until we get them back to the Gulch, do we? What would be the point of that?"

Another man stepped forward and said, "I object. Our orders were to convey Yaeger back to the Committee. Now that includes Brown. They both may have more information that needs to come out, and we weren't appointed to be executioners in any event. I don't want any part of that."

An uproar ensued among the men, and the subsequent argument became so heated that Williams was concerned that it might boil over into violence. He shouted above the arguing men, "Wait a minute! Calm down! Calm down! We can't have this type of behavior. I was also inclined to hang them, but now I've changed my mind. I want to take them to Alder Gulch and let the Committee deal with them. Settle down, everyone."

The men slowly began to calm themselves, and although there was grumbling and talk among them, the rest of the evening passed in relative peace.

The trip to Alder Gulch required one more layover at the trading post known as Laurin, located in the shadow of three large, steep mountains and next to a stream called the Stinking Water River. The group, now with the addition of Brown, rode hard and reached the post at dusk.

The station at Laurin had the advantage of containing two small rooms and a large one that served as the main area for eating, drinking, and rest. The prisoners were put into one of the small rooms under guard, and Williams took the other small room to take a nap. He had been sleeping soundly for an hour when a loud knocking awakened him. Groggy, he said, "Who's there? I'm trying to get a bit of rest for goodness' sake."

Outside the door, a man replied, "Look, Williams, you need to come quick. There's a problem. The men have been talking about the situation with Yaeger and Brown and want to hang them now. They seem like they mean to do it. They're worried about being ambushed on the trail by friends of Brown and Yaeger who'll come to try and free them."

Williams rose slowly from his bed on the floor, opened the door, and followed the man back into the station's main room. Once there, he addressed the men. "What's going on, gentlemen? I thought we'd decided to take Yaeger and Brown to Alder Gulch. I have been told that you now want to hang them. Let it be known that I am not in favor."

One of the men called out from the back of the room, "We need to get this over with now, Williams. No more waiting, and to hell with the Committee. That's what I think. According to you, Brown and Yaeger have already confessed. If they are part of a group of road agents, it is likely that word is already out that they've been captured. There is too much risk that somebody might try to free them before we get to Alder Gulch. So, I'm afraid we will get this done whether you go along or not."

The rest of the men voiced their approval, and Williams could see that they meant business. He realized that his authority had run its course and that it might be dangerous to push the men further. Williams thought for a moment and said, "All right, men. I can see you have a plan and nothing will change your minds. Let's go ahead and hang them, get it over with. We will do it in the morning but we need some rest for now. This has been a hard trip."

Yaeger and Brown were sleeping when Williams and two men entered their room. They were roused from their sleep, and sat up, bleary-eyed. As Yaeger began to awaken fully, he looked up at Williams and saw the look on his face. "It's time, isn't it? It's over for me," he said.

Williams nodded. "Yes, Red. I'm afraid the time has come. If there is anything else you want to confess, now is the time to do it."

Yaeger lowered his head. "I've done a lot

to deserve hanging, but if I'm going to hang, I want the others involved to hang too."

"What others, Red?"

Yaeger looked back up at Williams. "We are all part of a group of highwaymen. We relieve people of their gold when possible. We will also rustle horses and take anything of value. Rob stagecoaches or wagons. Ives was in on it. Me. Brown. Others too. And I'm sorry to say, the leader is Sheriff Plummer over in Bannack, and he has his deputies in on it. We operate all around this area from Bannack to the Gulch."

Williams looked surprised.

"*Sheriff Plummer?* Are you sure? Give me the names of the others."

"Hell yeah, I'm sure. The Sheriff put me onto an old man carrying gold from Bannack to Salt Lake City. I heard he was to leave out with a group of freighters, but then the damn fool set out by himself. He was easy pickings for us. We way laid him and got away with everything. Gold. Horse. Everything. I can give you all the names of the people in the gang if you have something to write on. Every single one of them."

"You can write?"

"Sure. I can write. My folks were good people, and I was able to get some education as a youngster. But then I drifted west and fell into wickedness. Now look where I am. It has all come to a bad end just like my old man told me it would."

Yaeger was given a piece of paper and some charcoal. He spent a few minutes writing down names, and then handed the paper to Williams, who studied the writing and then said to Yaeger and Brown, "Are you men ready?" Yeager nodded, but Brown did nothing and seemed to be looking somewhere far beyond the confines of the small room.

They moved Yaeger and Brown into the main room, waiting while Williams and the men discussed a suitable place for hanging their prisoners. Several strong cottonwood trees behind the station next to the Stinking Water River would work well for the hanging, noted Williams.

They deemed this place suitable, discovering a couple of large crates to provide a drop. The men led Yaeger and Brown to the cottonwood tree closest to the station house. There, they prepared the ropes, binding both men's arms tight to their bodies, and Brown was the first one they placed atop a crate, tightening a noose around his neck.

Williams said, "Do you have any last thing to say, Brown? Any final words to your loved ones?"

Brown was shaking. "I...I don't know. Loved ones...no. But will it hurt?"

"They say it doesn't hurt. It will be quick, son."

Brown turned his head slightly to look at the river. "I don't know why they call it the Stinking Water River. It doesn't smell that bad."

Williams nodded to a man standing next to the crate on which Brown stood, and the man quickly kicked it out from underneath him before Brown could even think of what was coming to him. Once Brown's body quit twitching and grew still, they pulled him down, limp and heavy, immediately replacing his body with Yaeger, a noose fixed around his neck. He glanced at Brown's body and said, "That was a strange thing for Brown to say."

Williams replied, "He was just scared.

That's all. Do you have anything you would like to say, Red?"

Yaeger looked over at a cottonwood tree several feet away. "Will you bury me in the shade of a cottonwood tree? Put Brown next to me, so I have a companion. You know, it sure is pretty country around here. I never thought much about that until now."

Williams smiled. "Yes, it is grand country, Red. Truly. I will make sure to bury you under a cottonwood. You have my word."

With that, Yaeger jumped off the crate to his death.

After the hanging of Yaeger and Brown, the group hurried on to Alder Gulch. When they arrived, each man went his own way, and Williams stopped in at Lott Saddlery. He needed to speak with Justin Lott, one of the leaders of the Vigilance Committee. Upon entering the workshop, he saw Lott busy at a workbench. Without looking up, Lott said, "I will be with you in just a moment. I need to finish something."

"I'm back, Lott. I will take a seat here while you finish." Williams sat in a chair close to Lott.

Lott looked up quickly and stopped

working. "Williams, good to see you. You look like you came through your journey in good shape. How did it go? Do you have Yaeger?"

"We had a problem with Yaeger on the trail. We had to hang him at the Laurin station, and we did the same to one of his fellow road agents. A man named Brown."

"Damn. You know the Committee wanted to question him in person. Did you get anything out of him?"

"We did get information. Yaeger admitted to being part of an organized group of road agents operating from Bannack to Alder Gulch, just as we suspected. Sheriff Plummer in Bannack is the leader, and there are many others in the gang. Before we hung him, Yaeger wrote the names down on a piece of paper."

"My goodness! Sheriff Plummer? Well, that's a surprise. I wouldn't have thought that. The situation is more serious than I believed. Do you have the paper with the names on it right now?"

"Yeah. I have it. Here, take it." Williams reached into a pocket of his coat, took out the paper, and handed it to Lott.

Lott studied the paper. "This is quite a list of people. You did a fine job. I will call a meeting and present this to the Committee. We will put an end to the work of these scoundrels. Go get some rest, and I will contact you soon."

Lott and Williams shook hands, and Williams departed. Lott stopped work for the day and tidied up his shop. He locked up the place and set out to contact the other members of the Vigilance Committee.

6

THE HANGING

January 10th, 1864, and Wichita stood at the bar in Durant's Saloon. He had been there for several hours, seeking warmth from the bitter cold outside. He had paced his drinking to remain relatively sober. Good conversation and a little gambling helped to pass the time.

Overall, the day had been uneventful and pleasant, and some might even have called it slow. At least as slow as a saloon could be in a mining town. There had been no fights and no brandishing of weapons, only the usual boisterous behavior.

Wichita stood back and admired the ornately carved bar, a defining feature of Durant's. That, and the nice facade on the front of the building with its two large windows containing multiple panes of rolled glass. It was rumored that Durant, the owner, had won the bar in a poker game and that the bartender had also been part of the bet.

The bartender never denied this, so it was taken as fact. Townspeople said that the bar had been cut into three pieces, transported by wagon to Bannack, and then reassembled in the bar. The rest of the bar was plain, made up of weathered chairs and tables, a large stove to provide heat, and two gaming tables to complete the interior.

One of the Sheriff's deputies, Ned Ray, had also spent the better part of the day in the saloon drinking. Ray had gone from slight drunkenness to belligerent bragging and finally to sleep as the day wore on. He was sleeping at one of the gaming tables, sitting in a chair with his head resting on the tabletop. Wichita looked over at Ray and shook his head in disgust. He then looked at the bartender.

"Damn," he said. "I sure am happy that he decided to take a nap. I like him a whole lot better when he's sleeping."

The bartender laughed and nodded his head in agreement.

The day was getting late, and Wichita was about to leave when several armed men burst through the door, leveling pistols and shotguns at everyone in the saloon.

A man moved to the center of the bar, announcing in a loud voice, "My name is Justin Lott, and I represent the Vigilance Committee. We formed up in Alder Gulch to rid our communities of dangerous criminals. We are here for Ned Ray. No one else. We have recruited sufficient men to stop anyone who tries to interfere. We shall also be arresting Sheriff Plummer and Buck Stinson, and we intend to hang them all today. Don't interfere, or things will go badly for you."

This announcement stunned Wichita; he had seen plenty of strange things in the camps over the years, but never had he heard of anyone hanging an elected sheriff. This would be a first, and a truly unpleasant one.

Wichita looked at Lott and said, "What's this? Hanging Sheriff Plummer and his deputies? What did they do? Aren't you going to at least give them a trial?"

Lott leveled his pistol at Wichita. "Be quiet, mister. This matter doesn't concern you. If you protest anymore, you might be joining the Sheriff at the end of a rope."

Wichita looked away and took a drink of whiskey as if Lott had said nothing, but his face was one of anger and disbelief.

Lott looked over at Ray passed out at the table, having barely moved since all the commotion in the bar started. Lott pointed to two men in his group. "You two men guard Ray," he instructed. "Let him sleep for now. We'll rouse him when the others get across the bridge from Yankee Flats with Sheriff Plummer and Stinson."

Lott pointed to another man. "You go just outside the door and keep a lookout for the others."

The man walked to the door, opened it, and went outside. Lott followed him with his eyes. After the man took up his position, Lott addressed the saloon. "All right. Everybody sits tight. We will let you go when the others get back with Sheriff Plummer and Stinson. You are then free to join us at the gallows."

Time passed slowly as everyone waited. Ray continued in his drunken sleep, oblivious to his fate. Suddenly, the man outside entered the saloon and excitedly said, "Lott, I can see them coming across Yankee Flats. Looks like they got both of 'em."

Lott looked at the men guarding Ray and said, "Okay. Get him on his feet and bind him."

He tossed a piece of rope to one of the men who abruptly jerked Ray to his feet, and before he could react, they pinned his arms. Others stepped forward and assisted in restraining Ray, quickly tying his arms in front, above his elbows.

Ray began to wake and regain his senses. He blurted out, "Hey...What in the hell are you doing? Untie me. I am a deputy in this town. You can't do this to me."

Lott walked up to Ray, who had begun to struggle, and said, "There is no use struggling Ray. The Vigilance Committee has decided your fate. You are going to hang today."

Ray was furious and struggled harder. "Hang? Vigilance Committee? You and your committee can go to hell. You can't hang me, you worthless bastards. I am the law in this town. Where is Sheriff Plummer?"

Lott lowered his head and shook it. "It

is over, Ray. Stop with the struggling. It won't do you any good. Your time would be better spent making peace with your maker."

Lott turned to the rest of his men and said, "Let's get him outside and wait for the others." Lott then told the saloon patrons they were free to go, and the group left the bar with Ray in tow, kicking at and cursing his captors.

Wichita followed the men and Ray outside. He looked across to Yankee Flats and saw a large group of men heading in the direction of the saloon. The gallows were located a few hundred yards directly behind Durant's, and Wichita figured the group was heading straight for it.

He remembered that Sheriff Plummer had ordered the gallows constructed only a few months before in order to hang a man who had robbed and murdered a miner. Wichita thought it strange that the rogue sheriff would soon be hanging from the gallows he had built himself. He could not see Sheriff Plummer or Stinson in the mass of men coming his way. His only thought was to get José and bring him back to witness the spectacle. The sun was beginning to set, and soon it would be dark.

When Wichita arrived at the door of José's cabin, he began banging frantically on it. He called out, "José! José! Come quickly. Something is going on down below. Men are trying to hang the Sheriff and his deputies." In a moment, the door opened, and José appeared. José calmly said, "Hello, Wichita. What is the commotion all about?"

"José, we need to get down the hill. Some men came into Durant's while I was there and took Ned Ray. They said they were part of some committee and that they were going to hang him. They got Sheriff Plummer and Stinson too. There are armed men all over Bannack right now, and they look to be heading for the gallows. Hurry! We have to go."

José looked shocked. "Sheriff Plummer and his deputies? That doesn't make any sense. The townspeople elected him. What did they do? Let me get my coat and hat."

José quickly grabbed his coat and hat. Both men started down the hill into town. It was close to dark, but they could see the large group moving toward the gallows.

Some in the crowd had lit torches, and the light bobbed up and down in the growing darkness. As José hurried toward the group, he thought about his interactions with Sheriff Plummer, drinking and talking about the old days. The Sheriff was a pleasant and good-mannered man, he thought. Not an angel for sure, but who was in the camps? José looked over at Wichita and said,

"Wichita, are you sure they mean to hang Sheriff Plummer and his deputies? I have never heard of such a thing. Of course, I have seen vigilante hangings in the camps, but never any sheriff. Did they say why they are doing this? Sure, Stinson and Ray are both unpleasant men, but you don't hang a man because he is unpleasant. I even get a little wild myself when I drink too much. That's just life in the camps, you know."

"I don't know, José. They just came in Durant's, held everyone at gunpoint, and said they were taking Ray. They didn't do any explaining. I've heard rumors of vigilantes ever since they hung that man in Alder Gulch for killing a boy last month. I heard his name was Ives."

"I heard about that too, but you hear all

kinds of things in Durant's. But didn't they give that man a miner's trial? Surely they won't hang someone without a trial."

Wichita grimaced. "It may be unfair, and it may be crazy, but you need to understand there isn't going to be any trial. They mean to hang these men right now. Never have I seen men more determined to see a thing through."

"This is crazy. More than that—it's unjust. Maybe we can convince others to join us and hold a miner's court."

"José, if you would let me give you a little advice, I wouldn't say anything. The man in charge, Lott, seemed damned determined, and they have a lot of men on their side right now. He threatened to stretch me just for asking about their actions. It's far too dangerous to do anything. It would have to come to a fight, and I don't think we can get enough people on our side to even things out."

"I don't like this at all, Wichita."

"I don't think liking it or not liking it has much to do with anything. All we can do now is see how this pans out."

By the time José and Wichita reached

Durant's, the crowd had already begun to move up the gully behind the saloon to the gallows. In the torchlight, they could see that the Sheriff, Stinson, and Ray were being herded like cattle, each one enclosed in a small circle. Ned Ray, now sufficiently sobered up and fully realizing his predicament, was hurling insults and curses at the men pushing him forward. Stinson walked along as though he were part of the group.

Sheriff Plummer could be seen moving to and fro in his circle, pleading his case to anyone who would listen. Despite it all, nothing stopped the silent forward motion of the crowd to the gallows. José and Wichita rushed to join it.

When the crowd reached the gallows, a large circle soon formed around it, pushing the doomed men to the middle. There was a heavy air of anticipation and a loud murmur in the crowd.

Lott stepped into the middle and raised his hand, signaling for silence. The murmuring group slowly became still. Lott addressed the crowd.

"Gentlemen, my name is Justin Lott, and I represent the Vigilance Committee. We formed the Committee in Alder Gulch and have sworn to rid the area of thieves, robbers, and murderers. We want to make this area safe and prosperous for everyone, and as you know, we have representatives here in Bannack where we have lately held an inquiry into the spate of robbery and murder that has taken place in this area. We have made a determination that the criminal behavior around here is due to an organized group of road agents.

"The leader of that group, I am deeply sorry to say, is Sheriff Plummer. His deputies are also involved. Thus, the Committee has sentenced the Sheriff and his deputies to death and has awarded me the task of carrying out that sentence. I intend to do it. We are engaged in a just cause and intend to harshly deal with anyone who attempts to interfere.

"Even as we stand here today, others are hunting and capturing additional members of the road agent group. We will punish these members just as severely in due haste."

Lott's speech caused an uproar in the crowd. Some began to question why there had been no public trial and no opportunity for the public to hear evidence against Sheriff Plummer and his deputies. The Sheriff took this as an opportunity to plead for a trial to prove his innocence.

Lott immediately called for the supporters of the Vigilance Committee to form an inner circle, and soon, they were pointing guns outward at those members of the crowd who still dared to protest the actions of Lott and the Committee. The uproar continued until Lott ordered his supporters to fire their guns in the air, bringing a swift silence over the crowd.

He then shouted to the group, "This matter is settled. Do you all wish to fight and possibly die over this? The men who have undertaken this task are upstanding citizens, fighting against the evils and untruths of a band of men who promised to protect you— yet who were committing heinous acts. We are working on your behalf to protect you and the women and children of this area. We don't act lightly, and we are willing to back up our decision by force if necessary.

"We will fulfill our task, one way or the other. Sheriff Plummer, Stinson, and Ray will die here today, and so will any who attempt to divert us from this, our solemn duty."

Tension and restlessness reigned among the crowd for several minutes.

Everyone calculated their course of action, waiting for someone else to act. Then, the group settled down as it became apparent that there was no point in the murmurings or cries of discontent; the decision was final. The terrible hanging would occur no matter what anyone said.

The Sheriff still moved back and forth across the circle, pleading for a trial, but now his pleas were falling on deaf ears. He looked pallid and sweaty, his eyes large and wild, tear laden.

Ray shook his head and looked upon the entire scene with contempt, while Stinson lowered his head and appeared to be praying silently. One young man rushed to the circle's center and hugged the Sheriff, sobbing and saying goodbye. Some of Lott's supporters roughly removed him, unnerving the Sheriff by this gesture. He continued to plea for a trial, but his voice cracked now, sounding shaky and uneven. Then suddenly, he stopped all his efforts as the moment of truth dawned: this was his final moment alive.

He stood up straight and fell silent.

Lott turned to some men in the circle and said, "It is time. Please assist with Ned Ray."

Four men stepped forward to help, quickly grabbing Ray and placing him under one of three prepared ropes. Ray did not even bother to struggle, no doubt realizing that it would do him no good, and perhaps resulting in less mercy if he could even hope for such a thing at the last moment. If being compliant and taciturn meant they were less rough in handling him, then it was for the best.

However, this did not keep him from continuing to curse and berate his captors.

Lott fixed the noose around his neck and said to the men, "Lift him high and give him a good drop." They lifted Ray as high as the men could manage and suddenly dropped him.

It did not go to plan. As he plummeted, Ray managed to slide some fingers between the noose and his neck. It had been a mistake to tie his hands in front, and this was now apparent. The fingers prevented his neck from breaking, and Ray began to strangle instead.

As Ray struggled, the torches created a scene where his face was sometimes in darkness and sometimes in light. His tortured face would suddenly appear to the crowd and then disappear. Back and forth. Red and swollen. Ray's eyes were wide and full of panic. His mouth struggled for air and only produced loud and raspy gasps in the cold night air.

The gasps were ever-present marking the time to his inevitable death. Exhalations of breath gave the gasps a misty, physical presence in the cold, little pieces of his soul escaping from a dying body. The crowd was silent as this macabre scene played itself out.

José whispered to Wichita, "This is barbaric. They need to get his fingers out and drop him again. We need to step in and tell them."

Wichita harshly whispered back to José, "You'll not be doing a damn thing now. Not if you value your life."

At first, Ray's gasps were strong and desperate, but then they became weaker, more time passing between them as his body started to succumb.

Legs that had been kicking wildly, trying to find purchase on ground that his feet could not reach, began to twitch weakly and then not at all. Ray took one large last gasp and fell still. Instead of all being over in the blink of an eye, it had taken several minutes for him to die suspended there, his body writhing, kicking and flailing while his face turned through a spectrum of colors and his mouth contorted, moans and huffs escaping in place of any final words.

In the end, blood was dripping from his mouth, ears and nose. These things would never happen if a hanging passed according to the plan. This one had gone wrong. No one should have had to witness such torment.

Lott seemed utterly unaffected by Ray's death, and in a businesslike manner, he directed the men to Stinson. Now, they did at least correct the mistake they had made with Ray.

They set about binding Stinson's arms behind his back, taking great care this time over the strength and formation of knots before repeating the same thing exactly with Sheriff Plummer. Neither man offered any protest, even though both had walked without restraint on their journey to the gallows. They had not allowed Ray to make a final statement, but Lott now gave that opportunity to Stinson.

Stinson thought briefly and said, "Do you want me to confess my crimes?"

Before anyone could respond, Sheriff Plummer shouted out, "What the hell do you want to confess, Stinson? We've both done enough in our lives to deserve this. Everyone here deserves the end of a rope. Be quiet. Do you hear me? You can confess to your maker or tormentor when you get where you're going. I don't want to wait all day for my turn."

Stinson looked hard at the Sheriff, then lowered his head and said, "I'm ready."

They moved him to a rope next to the now dead Ray, fixing the noose in place around his neck. Then they lifted him high and dropped him. Stinson died with hardly a twitch.

Now it was the Sheriff's turn. He was calm, walking willingly to his place beneath the last rope. Lott gave him a chance to speak. The Sheriff swallowed hard, looked out at the crowd, and then seemed to look beyond.

He said loudly and firmly, "I say goodbye to those who know me and are my friends. They know my true character. I wish things hadn't turned out this way. I don't feel that I deserve this treatment, but I see you mean to hang me. It seems a strange way for it all to end. Just give me a good drop like Stinson. That's all I ask of you now."

They raised the Sheriff like the others, dropped him, watching him die immediately. The crowd slowly dispersed, leaving the three men hanging and swaying in the dark.

José and Wichita walked reflexively back toward Durant's. At first, they moved in stunned silence, as did most of the others leaving the gallows. But then, José suddenly looked over at Wichita and said, "This is madness. How can we live around people like this? Who are these men to make this decision? We need to get out of here. Quick."

Wichita nodded in approval. "It's as bad as I've seen, that's for sure. The situation could turn in any direction now. Believe me, I've seen it happen more than once in my time. After a while, they start hanging any-body they don't like. You'll soon see."

He carried on muttering and mumbling to himself for quite some time, prophesying doom, staring at the ground as they walked. Whether his companion was even listening was another matter; he too had lost himself in his own melancholy thoughts.

They arrived at Durant's and went inside, trying to relax while still pondering their sit-uation. Wichita paid for a bottle of whiskey. The mood in the saloon was subdued, and voices were low, creating a soft background murmur. José and Wichita spent most of their time in silence, deep in thought, each considering their options—not that options were exactly plentiful.

They talked a little about rumors of other gold strikes they could move to and work, but there was none of the usual enthusiasm accompanying such talk. Eventually, they shook hands, said goodnight, and departed.

$\sim$

LOTT KNOCKED on the door of Randall Sanders' cabin later that night. Sanders answered the door and said, "Hello, Lott. It's been a hell of a day. Come in and warm yourself by the stove. How can I be of assistance?"

Both men moved into the cabin, grabbed chairs, and sat down by the stove.

Lott warmed his hands. "We still have some unfinished business."

Sanders looked at Lott. "What do you mean?"

"I'm talking about Greaser Joe. We need to figure out what we are to do with him."

"Greaser Joe? Oh, you mean the Mexican in town—the one named José, right?"

"Yeah him. There's some information that he's been drinking and hanging around with the Sheriff and his bunch in Durant's. Not just that, but he did it on more than one occasion. Can't say as I feel easy about it under the circumstances, you know?"

"Oh, come on. So what? What 'circumstances' do you mean? Many people in town have had drinks and talked with Sheriff Plummer in Durant's. You're going to think every person who ever had a drink with the Sheriff is suddenly on the wrong side of the law?"

"No, I didn't say that. I'm talking about Greaser Joe. People say he's a rough man and no good. Well, let's face it, greasers are *usually* no good and they're involved in crime more often than not. We need to talk to him and see if he has any useful information. The Sheriff might have brought him in on some of the robbery and murder around here."

Sanders shook his head. "This is no good. Do we have any evidence, besides gossip, that José might be involved in road agent activities? Everyone is rough in Bannack. Including you. That's how things are in a mining camp."

"The accusations are enough. Besides, we need to rid our communities of these undesirable types. How does having a greaser benefit this area? Tell me that."

Sanders pointed at Lott. "Look, I don't know where you're coming from. He's a man like any other. He has rights. What do you want to do after you question him? Banish him?"

"Maybe. We need to get a bunch of men together and go up to his cabin. Then what happens after that happens."

"It sounds like you want to do this man

in, kill him, regardless of what he has or hasn't done. I don't know that I agree with that type of thinking."

Lott rolled his eyes. "Get some courage, Sanders. No matter what you say, he *is* just a greaser. If we just put up with his sort, it will send a strong message to the undesirable types that they can do as they please, and I personally can't be having that. So, I've already made some arrangements for the morning.

"We will go up to his cabin at first light. Why do you even care what happens to him? You need to get over it because all I know is that it won't look good to the men if you don't show up at the cabin. They might think you're trying to protect the greaser. You're a representative of the Vigilance Committee in this town."

Sanders gave Lott a disgusted look. "You're a bastard Lott. But all right. I'll be there."

Lott smiled. "Good. As I said before, we leave at first light. I'll come over here and get you, and you better dress for warmth. It is going to be cold. Now, get some sleep."

Lott got up, shook hands with Sanders,

and left. Sanders continued to sit by the stove, extracting all the warmth he could from it. Slumped in his chair, a look of sadness came across his face. He knew the danger of going against Lott and the others, and he was disgusted with what might happen in the morning. The vision of Ned Ray slowly strangling, his eyes popping out of his head, was still fresh in his mind.

7

DEATH

A righteous mob flows over the land like a giant wave, scouring away everything in its path. When it recedes, there is nothing left but death and destruction.

IT WAS EARLY in the morning, just after daybreak, when they came. The sun had just begun to spread a little warmth over the frozen land. The mob moved toward the cabin in silence, the crunch of the snow beneath their feet marking their tempo. Arriving at the cabin, they surrounded it and waited for the leaders to act.

The cold felt less intense in anticipation of what was to come. The leaders, Lott and Sanders, were huddling together for a conference. Sanders rubbed his hands against one another, cupped them to his mouth, and tried to blow warmth into them. It barely worked since the morning hours were frigid. He lowered his hands and said to Lott, "We can't stand around much longer. I'm too cold for that. So, how do you want to handle this, Lott?"

"I don't know. Let's give him a chance to surrender first. He's done for either way."

Sanders looked at Lott. "Surrender? Once he realizes all the men are out here, I'm inclined to think he won't surrender. He'll know what awaits him. I think we'll have to root him out of there."

"Hell, Sanders. Let's give him a chance, can't we? If he surrenders, we might be able to question him a little bit and get some information. Then we can turn him over to the others and let them take care of him. We will take care of him if he doesn't surrender right here. Plus, if we can get him to surrender, we can avoid getting any of the men hurt."

"Information?" Sanders shook his head

in disgust. "What information? We have no reason to believe he had anything to do with the Sheriff and that bunch. It doesn't seem right to me. So, he drinks with him once in a while. He hasn't done anything to deserve what's going to happen."

"Sanders, listen to me. These greasers aren't good for a town trying to become respectable. Bannack has a future other than picking gold out of the ground. We need a place where god-fearing folks can live in peace and prosperity. We have to get rid of the criminals and undesirable types."

"Does that include that Shoshone girl you visited at the brothel when you got to town?"

"Be careful what you say, Sanders. Don't go soft on me now. After what's happened here and what will happen, the men might take your softness the wrong way. They might think you are trying to protect some of these criminals and undesirables. Anything can happen right now. You know what I mean, don't you?"

Sanders kicked at the snow with his boot, grimacing. "Do whatever the hell you want, Lott. It doesn't matter now. We're in too deep after the Sheriff. This mess all has to go to its conclusion."

Lott looked hard at Sanders and then yelled out, "Greaser Joe. Come out. We need to talk to you." No sound came from the cabin. He yelled out again.

"Greaser, come out and surrender now. If you come out, I promise we'll go easy on you. We have the place surrounded. Don't make me have to send men in after you."

Again, there was silence. Lott threw his hands up and looked around at the assembled men. He said in a loud voice, "Shit. I guess this is going to get done the hard way. I need a couple of volunteers to go in and see if the damn greaser is even in there. Any volunteers?"

Smith Ball and George Copley stepped forward. Ball said, "We'll go in there and dig that bastard out." Lott nodded to the men. "Good. Get to it, gentlemen."

It was dark in the cabin. It was not the case that José was avoiding answering the calls to him. He was not refusing to come out or taking any actions to hide himself away.

No. He was simply asleep and dreaming, inside his own head, knowing not a thing about what was going on outside his door. In his dream, he was standing at the doorway of an old adobe house, trying to see inside, but there was only blackness.

A hot wind swirled dust at his feet. José awoke to yelling coming from outside. In his grogginess, he could not make out what the words even were or who was speaking them. Once his senses cleared, he realized that someone was calling for him to go outside and surrender. He was confused but immediately recognized the danger.

Fear started to take hold in the pit of his stomach, spreading fast to the rest of his body, making his arms and legs tense and heavy.

What's happening? Why is someone here wanting me to surrender? I have done nothing to warrant people being here, calling out to me like that.

Outside, the men were only becoming more aggravated and annoyed, building up more venom and loathing. The longer they called and got no response, the more annoyed they became, the pressure building up like a pot left too long on the stove, rising ready to boil over.

José could hear the voices more clearly now, and he fumbled for his revolver, his hands also heavy and slow due to fear. It was easy to find as he always kept the gun close. He tried to grab clothes quickly but could not locate any due to the darkness adding to his panic.

Maybe they only want to talk. No. Men who want you to surrender never come just to talk, do they? I don't want this to happen to me. There must be many men out there, a group like the one that came for Sheriff Plummer yesterday. I don't have much time and have to think of something to do. Six shots. That is all I have for them.

There is nothing I can do with six shots. I can get a couple of them, maybe. What else is there to do? I was living in peace here. I did nothing. Damn them.

José located some clothes and tried to put them on, but he was too stiff and scared to succeed. His feet were ending up in the same pant leg, then he fell over. His failure to dress made him laugh, but then he cried, fat tears tolling down both cheeks.

For God's sake. I can't even dress myself now. They're going to force their way in and slaughter

*me in my underwear, collapsed on the god-
damned floor, all twisted up in my clothes.*

*What dignity is there in that? To hell with it.
I'm going to shoot it out the best I can. Plus, I'll
save a bullet for myself.*

*I'm not going to die by the rope. Nope. Make
sure you shoot yourself before they get the gun. I
need to get into that corner. That will give me a
good angle when they come through the door.*

*I will get in the corner and put the bed in
front of me, piling the bedding up. It will hide me
a little bit. I need to move the bed. Be quiet.*

José quickly moved the bed to form a
barrier in front of the corner. He piled up the
bedding, crawled over the bed, and hunched
down in the corner. He pulled back the bed
toward him to rest his gun hand on it. José
cocked his revolver and waited for the men
to come through the door.

Outside, Lott gestured to Ball and Copley.
He pointed to the door of the cabin and said,
"Get moving, gentlemen. It's cold out here.
The sooner we get this done, the sooner we
can get someplace warm. He's just a greaser,
probably won't even put up much of a fight.
Let's get it over with."

Ball gave Lott a look of disbelief. "I don't

know about that, Lott. I've seen some tough greasers in my day." Ball then looked at Copley and said, "Let's go then, Copley."

The two men cautiously approached the cabin door, guns drawn. Ball banged on the door and said, "Anybody in there? Come out now." He waited, and after there was no response, he put his ear to the door and listened for sound inside. Ball put his hand on the door handle, rattling it up and down to test if it would open or whether it would put up a fight of its own. They might have to kick down the door.

He motioned for Copley to come near him and then whispered in his ear, "Okay, I'm going to open this door and go to the left. It feels like it will open. You go to the right. Got it? Are you ready?"

Copley nodded that he understood and waited for Ball to make his move. Ball quickly opened the door and entered. Copley followed right behind him and stepped to the right. Neither man could see anything when they entered the cabin due to the sudden change from light to darkness. In the corner, José could see them.

Two quick shots came from inside the

cabin. The men outside instantly became alert at the sound. They raised guns, pointing toward the dwelling. Ball and Copley stumbled out into the daylight, staggering and lurching as though both men had entered sober but now were drunk. Ball screamed, "I'm shot! The greaser's in there, and that bastard's shot me in the hip. Somebody come here and help."

Copley stopped, hung his head, and croaked, "I can't. I'm dying."

He coughed up a large amount of blood, took a few steps, and collapsed on the ground. There was no attempt to break the fall, and he landed face-first on the frozen ground with a loud thud.

Ball hobbled over to Copley, sat down next to him, announcing, "Shit. Copley is dead." Ball leaned back and laid his head on the ground. He placed his hand on his bleeding hip. Lott, Sanders, and several other men rushed to Ball's side. Lott looked down at Ball.

"How bad off are you, Ball?"

Ball grimaced in pain. "I can make it for a while. Do you have anything to use for a bandage? I'm bleeding pretty bad but I'm not leaving until that bastard's dead. I can't believe Copley's gone. The greaser put an end to him."

The men helped Ball move to a spot safely away from the cabin, bandaging Ball's wound as best they could and seeing that although it was painful, Ball was in no immediate danger from it. They then carried Copley's body to a location a few feet from Ball. Lott and Sanders stood together, looking at Ball, worry on each man's face.

Lott spoke first and said, "Well, that didn't work. What do we do now? It looks like the greaser means to make a fight of it. We can't risk more men getting shot, or this deal might turn against us."

Sanders replied, "Yeah. I agree. It's a damn shame what happened to Copley." The men stood in silence for a moment, and then Sander's face brightened. He exclaimed, "I have an idea. Judge Edgerton has a mountain howitzer that he hauled out here. I believe he even has some powder and exploding shot for it. It isn't that large, weighs just a bit more than a large man, two hundred pounds or so if I remember correctly. Let's get it. Then, we can shoot the cabin and not risk the men. It ought to do the trick."

Lott looked at Sanders incredulously. "What makes you think the Judge will give us the howitzer? Especially when we tell him we're trying to shoot someone with it."

"What is he going to do, Lott? We'll take the howitzer from him. The Judge saw what happened here yesterday. He doesn't have anyone to back him. Formal law has broken down now. He might be the Judge around here, but *we* are the law now."

"You're right, Sanders. We are the law. We'll round up enough of these men to haul the howitzer. The rest can guard the cabin on the chance that the greaser might decide to shoot his way out. Let's get going."

Lott and Sanders quickly put their plan into action. They assembled the group they wanted for the howitzer and left for Judge Edgerton's house, an ominous stillness settling over the scene.

Inside the cabin, José sat waiting, bracing for a sudden rush of men. None came. Minutes passed in anticipation and tension.

I hit both of them. One of them pretty good, I think. Four shots left. Three for them and one for me. *I wish I could close that door, but I don't dare go near it. Can't risk it.*

What's going on out there? I thought they'd have rushed in here by now. They must be making another plan. Well, make your damn plans. It all ends the same anyway. There's a bottle of whiskey over there on the table. I need to get it. I don't think they'll be able to see me. I just need a few drinks. It will help.

José slowly got up, crawled over the bed, and quickly retrieved the bottle of whiskey. He then barricaded himself back into the corner, uncorking the bottle and greedily taking a long drink. The whiskey burned on his tongue, and he relished the taste.

Ah, that tasted good. Very good. Maybe they've changed their minds and they might decide to leave me alone. No, don't think that way; what would be the point in it?

These kinds of men don't change their minds; more likely, they'll try to burn me out. That one is easy because I swear I'll shoot myself before I burn. I could try to make a run for it. Try to get to the creek, grab a horse and get out of town. Nope. There's too much open ground and too many of them. They might get me alive and give me the rope. I don't want to die that way.

Shit. I just have to make sure I don't get the rope!

I'm so damn scared, not ready for it to end, but I guess you never are ready for it. There's only one way out, and I have to accept it.

But they won't get me; I'm still the one in control because they can't stop me choosing how I go. They haven't taken that from me yet, and I'll have to make sure they don't take it from me too.

No matter what, I need to get a couple more of them anyway, give them something to remember.

The group of men arrived at Judge Edgerton's house sitting on the main street of Bannack. It was one of the more robustly built buildings in town, not one that had been thrown up in a hurry like other buildings, but it wasn't ornate or fancy since the Judge fancied himself as a practical and down-to-earth person.

Lott went up to the door and knocked on it. A young woman answered, and Lott said, "Miss, would Judge Edgerton be available now?"

"May I tell him who's calling? There appears to be something going on up on the hill over there." She pointed in the direction from which Lott had just come. "After yesterday, things are just frightful."

"Yes, Miss. There is a situation developing up on the hill. The Judge's assistance is needed immediately. Please tell him that Mr. Lott is here to see him."

"I will get the Judge right now."

The woman disappeared into the house while the men stood outside. Soon, the gaunt and tall figure of Judge Edgerton appeared at the door. He looked at the assembled men, then to Lott, and said, "Good morning, gentlemen. Lott, what brings you here on this rather frigid morning?"

Lott appeared fidgety. "We've run into a bit of a problem up on the hill, Judge. We took a group of men up to Greaser Joe's place to question him on the orders of the Vigilance Committee. He decided to shoot it out with us, and killed a man named Copley, wounding another.

"He's holed up in his cabin and won't come out. We need to borrow your mountain howitzer to end this situation without any more men getting hurt. This greaser is tough to deal with and won't see reason. Well, same as they all are, I suppose."

Judge Edgerton rubbed his chin.

"Lott, I am sure few men will see reason if they think you're about to send them to meet their maker. After the business with Sheriff Plummer and his deputies, I suspect this man was scared. He probably saw Sheriff Plummer stretched yesterday and thought you were about to do the same thing to him. I guess you can have the howitzer. It would be best to get this taken care of before anyone else gets hurt. I haven't thrown in with the Vigilance Committee, but I know I can't stop it. I'll show you where the howitzer and supplies are located. Follow me. Oh, do you mind if I come along to watch? I haven't seen the howitzer being fired in some time."

Lott raised an eyebrow and looked at the Judge. "Uh... Sure, Judge. You are welcome to come along if you want."

Edgerton directed the men to the howitzer and necessary supplies, and soon they were on their way, rushing back to the cabin as fast as they could travel with their new implement.

Arriving at their destination, Lott had the

men place the howitzer on a large wooden box, and the men aimed the barrel at a side of the cabin. Edgerton helped direct the loading of powder and shot. When they were ready to fire the howitzer, Lott stepped forward to direct the action.

He raised an arm and quickly dropped it. "Okay, gentlemen. Let it rip."

A loud crack and boom filled the air, a hole appearing in the side of the cabin, but nothing else happened. The shot had not detonated. Lott was unhappy and shouted, "It didn't explode. Let's send another in there."

A second shot fired. Again, a hole appeared in the cabin, but there was still no explosion. The dwelling was still intact, except for two big holes in it. Lott was now incensed, and he screamed, "That damn fool gave us defective shot. How are we supposed to finish this job if nothing works? The greaser is probably in there laughing at us. Move that howitzer and aim it at the chimney side this time. We're going to give this one more try."

They relocated the howitzer and aimed at the chimney, firing off the third shot.

Again, a crack and boom filled the air. But this time, there was a loud explosion, the cabin collapsing in on itself, sending a cheer up from the group of men. Lott now had a grin on his face. He shook the hand of the man nearest to him and said, "We got him. There is no way he made it through that one. Okay, we need to have a look. Everybody move forward but be careful. Remember, a rattlesnake can be the most dangerous when it's wounded."

José was on his back beneath the broken remains of the cabin. His breathing came quick and ragged, and coldness spread throughout his body. Blood, pain, and smoke were his only companions. He was stunned, and his ears were ringing. He could make out rays of light that penetrated the darkness, but that was all. As his head cleared a little, he realized that he was partially covered by debris and that his home had collapsed.

Suddenly, José felt someone take his hand. His body filled with warmth, and a face appeared before him. It was the young woman, Marina, looking down on him with concern and tenderness. José spoke to her in a raspy voice,

"How...How did you get here? You must leave quickly. It is too dangerous for you to be here. Go. You must go now."

Marina brushed bloody matted hair out of his eyes. "Be still. Everything is going to be okay. They can't hurt me. Be strong for a little while longer. It's almost over."

José became still and quiet, a hush coming over him as if she could quell the pain and fear in his soul with just a few words. He looked intensely into Marina's eyes, feeling that he was truly loved at that moment. He closed his eyes, took a deep breath, and opened them again. Marina was gone. José whispered, "Don't leave, Marina. I don't want to be alone."

Now, something or someone was dragging José by the feet. He could see the light and knew he was outside. But he was very weak and could not speak or resist. Unfamiliar faces looked down on him, everything seeming to occur in a foggy, dreamlike state. However, the pain and the taste of blood in his mouth let him know it was real and not a dream.

He did not feel fear now, though, and he was calm. The men stood looking at the injured man. Ball limped up to José, looked down, and said, "Hey, the greaser is still alive. It would have been better for him if death had come when we blew up his cabin. Oh well, I'll finish the job."

Ball gestured to the crowd of men. "Does anybody object to me finishing him right here and now? After all, he shot me and killed Copley. He's done for and in my opinion, not worth hanging. Maybe we'll hang him after he's dead and use him for target practice."

No one in the group of men objected or dared say anything. Judge Edgerton lowered his head and quietly and quickly walked away from the scene. Lott and Sanders stood by passively, silent. Ball looked around at the crowd, paused, drawing his revolver. He fired six shots into José.

José let the last breaths pass from his body, his heart and breathing constricting, field of vision narrowing until he no longer saw his tormentors. Bright blood pooled on the ground; he had bled out in a heartbeat. The last thing he saw was a bright, blue sky, and then the darkness came. Perhaps this was the best he could have hoped for; it was as merciful a death as a man could dream of, six shots in quick succession, following the sweet words of a girl who loved him.

When Wichita learned of the death of José, he rushed to the cabin, wanting to take control of the body and give him a proper burial. However, when he arrived, it was instantly clear this was not possible. The remains of the cabin had been set on fire, the body of José now resting atop it, carelessly thrown there by way of a further penance.

Wichita sat on the ground, weeping as the fire consumed José, erasing his existence from that world. Sally arrived later, but there was nothing left, only ashes and a few charred remains of wood. Wichita had told Sally about how José had burned with the cabin, how they had done that to him.

She scooped up a small amount of ash and placed it in a handkerchief, taking it back to the brothel and putting the ashes in a glass jar. Sally placed it on the highest shelf in the kitchen area. For the rest of her life, the jar traveled with her.

8

REBIRTH

Dust in light. Where am I? I fell asleep, that's all, and now I am here. What is that up ahead? I can see something.

José walked forward. At least it felt as though he was walking forward. There was no pain or fear now. He walked into the square of a small village that, at first, he did not recognize, and was able to see a small adobe house a short distance away.

Outside of the house, a girl was playing contentedly by a well, her back turned to him. The day was sunny and should have been hot, but he didn't feel any discomfort from the heat. This fact did not make an impression on him initially, the scene in front transfixing him.

This place looks familiar, like where I grew up. I can feel the wind, and it should be hot. But it's not hot, is it? I just don't feel it, yet I should. But I don't feel any more pain, and it hurt so bad before I fell asleep. I don't understand.

José decided to walk over to the girl and talk to her. She was young, and he judged her age not to be more than ten. He wanted to know where he was now. It seemed ridiculous; this was just a dream, wasn't it? It had to be. A pleasant dream, but a dream, nonetheless. When he got close to her, she straightened up but did not immediately turn to face him. She had long, black hair and wore a brightly colored dress.

Looking down at her, he said, "Hey, little one. Can you tell me where I am?"

The girl turned around and looked at José with a big smile. He was stunned by the sight of her and took a few steps backward.

"Oh! Marina. How can this be? It's been such a long time... I mean, it can't be. This doesn't make sense."

Marina burst out laughing. "Hello, brother. How are you on this fine day?"

"This can't be real. It must be a dream. You can't be this way after so many years."

"This place is more real than the one you just left."

Tears welled in his eyes, and he looked down at the ground. "I think I understand now."

Marina stood up and looked at José with concern. "Why are you sad? There's nothing to be sad about here. We're reunited at last, aren't we? Isn't this what we both wanted, brother? I, at least, have waited a lifetime for this."

"How can you have waited a lifetime?" He laughed. "You're barely old enough to be out alone."

"Is that so?" she said and giggled. "Well, to me, it seems as if I've been managing a lot better on my own than you have. And plus, time isn't what you think it to be, brother."

He looked at her, then at himself. He was in a sorry state, mixed up, confused. She was right though. How could it be that a slip of a girl could teach him about life, about what was real and what was just a nightmare? How could she know about time's reality, and about the illusion from which he appeared to have escaped?

José looked at her, sadness still in his eyes. A question came. In fact, many of them. "Whichever way you look at it, it's been so long. You look just like you did when I last saw you. Did it happen right after I left?"

"No. It didn't happen right away. It happened later when I was a young woman. I don't remember much about it to tell the truth. After you are here a while, you don't remember everything. Or maybe don't remember anything. It is nothing to be scared of. Some memories float by like clouds, and it's hard to grasp them. Other things I remember very well, and I don't know why. I think we keep the important memories, and our passing isn't important."

"No, you're right. It isn't. But what *is* important is that I am sorry I never came back. I should have come back to see you."

"Don't be sorry. It is what it is, and all things that have happened are gone now. We are here, and we are eternal. Time has no meaning here; we are part of one another and part of God."

"What do you mean we are part of God?"

"You are his expression, his thought, and he is in you. We all come from the stars and the deep night sky. Water and earth. Flesh and blood. Things that last forever and things that pass. Things that remain and others that are transient. All times and all places are connected. And love. Love is eternal."

"Why do you look this age if it happened later? It was you I saw in Bannack then, was it? But I couldn't recognize you at the time. Are Mama and Papa here as well?"

"This world is as you expect it to be. Mama and Papa are here, but not *right* here. I look this way because that is how you remember me. When you saw me in the other world, you saw me how I was when I passed from that world, but I was there to guide you."

José looked around.

"Everything is exactly as I remember it. Is it still just a short distance to the river?"

Marina smiled and rolled her eyes. "Yes. Just like it always was, brother."

"Let's go down there. Just like we used to."

They started walking toward the river.

José held Marina's hand as they walked, and he noticed that his hands looked younger, less worn from work. They arrived at the riverbank and went down a short, steep slope to the river's edge.

There, José picked up a rock and skipped it across the water where it bounced several times before disappearing beneath the surface. Marina clapped her hands with delight. José turned to her and said, "Do you remember when I taught you how to do that?"

"Yes, I remember. Give me a rock then."

She reached out her hand, and José placed a rock in it.

She wound up and skipped the rock with an exaggerated motion, probably for her brother's benefit, to make him laugh. The rock only took two bounces before disappearing beneath the water. Marina bent over with laughter.

"José, I think you gave me a rock that wasn't flat enough. It didn't skip very well. That must have been the problem. I swear you keep all the best rocks for yourself and always did."

José was laughing. "No. It was a good

rock. I guess I just didn't teach you very well."

"Yes. It was all your fault, brother, one way or the other."

"Marina, when you were very young, I would take you down here in the afternoons. I would pick up the largest rock I could find and throw it in the water to make a big splash. You would clap your hands with excitement. Then, you would pick up a rock and do the same thing after me. You would stand there and look around as though you were waiting for applause. I thought that was very funny."

Marina must have remembered that based on her flamboyant arm action when she'd wound the rock just now; she had done it all for her brother's benefit to take him back to the good times from their past. She seemed intent on taking his stress away, and so far, it was working.

They both laughed some more, then sat down close to the water. José and Marina removed their footwear and put their bare feet in the cold river, watching the slow-moving water. Occasionally, a piece of wood or some other debris would float by, and they would track its progress.

There was a comfortable silence between them, and both felt at peace. This silence went on for some time, then José looked over at his sister and said, "Sometimes, before, we just did what we are doing now. We would sit by the water, watching it pass by us, wonder where the things floating in it would end their journeys. We were together, even though it didn't seem like much.

"They were such simple things, you know... simple pleasures in life, ones we didn't fully understand or appreciate at the time. The smell of Mama's cooking, Papa's laughter at a joke, celebrations with family and friends. I am thinking about these things now. I was a wanderer, loving the adventure, but I never knew where it was that I wanted to go. I am sorry I missed so much time with you and things important to you. And Mama too."

"Brother, as I told you before, there is no need for sorrow anymore. Let go of it, please. We will always be together now, and time has no measure here."

He smiled, though a weak smile as if he

could not quite believe it could all be as easy as Marina was describing. Life—his old life —had not been kind to him.

"Do you remember that auburn-haired girl that I used to see before I left home? I brought her across the river one time, and you met her."

Marina thought about it a moment. "I cannot grasp that memory. I don't remember her. I am sorry."

He looked momentarily sad about even that.

"It's okay. Do you think she could be here? I mean... Can I cross this river?"

"Maybe she's here. I don't know. But yes, you can cross the river. This world will be as you want it to be. However, people will only be here if they've crossed into this world, and if they choose who they'll see or not see. If you think hard about them, they will know you are here."

"Marina, let's go back to the village. Are there any horses there? Can I see them?"

"I bet there is a fine horse to be found in the village and everything you need to ride it."

"Good. Let's go."

They walked back to the village, and when they reached the edge of it, Marina turned to José and said, "If you go behind that building over there, you will find a horse."

She pointed the way. José looked at her as though he didn't quite believe what she'd said. But he decided to look and see if she was right. He set off for the building, and when he arrived behind it, there was indeed a small corral. In the corral was a fully saddled and outfitted horse as if it was waiting for him. He entered the corral, went up to the horse, and mounted it. The horse did not flinch at his approach or touch, and it did not try to move away when mounted.

José nodded his head in approval and said, "A horse that stands still when you get on it. I might grow to like this place." He started the horse back toward where he'd left Marina.

José rode up to Marina, still standing in the same spot where he had seen her last. She looked up at him, her eyes bright and sparkling. Her head was a little tilted to one side, her arms crossed, and she had a knowing look. José looked down at her and said, "If it's all the same to you, I think I'll take a ride across the river and see who is on the other side. It will only be a short ride, mind you, and won't be too long. Who knows, maybe Margaret is on the other side. Oh, that was the name of the girl I brought across the river, you know." José paused. "Will I see you again, Marina?"

He looked at her with hope in his eyes, also the familiar glimmer of sadness and doubt. Perhaps he was a little afraid of riding away in case he were to lose her a second time.

Marina smiled at him with affection. "Think about me, and I will come. Have a safe journey, José. Wherever you travel, just remember, I am there, and I love you. So, it doesn't matter how far away you are or how long it takes to return. You should learn not to worry about such things. We are together always."

José looked at her, too afraid to leave or speak. Then he relaxed and said, "I know, and I love you too, sister."

She was wise and right; life had parted them before—for a long time—and yet there she was, barely a whisper or a breath away, unchanged from the last time they had stood opposite one another. He had only to call out to her, and she would be here for him.

He turned his horse away from her and started toward the river.

Now, José was smiling.

ACKNOWLEDGMENTS

It takes several people to publish a book. They are all important. I want to thank my wonderful editor, Annie, my book cover designer, Rose, and everyone else who contributed to the making of this book.